FALSE FLAG

FALSE FLAG

JAY TINSIANO

Dark Paradigm Publishing

ACKNOWLEDGEMENTS

Thanks to all the beta readers who helped improve False Flag. Also a special thanks to Cate Hogan for her editing work, Jay Newton for his valuable contribution and all those who encouraged me to stay on track.

If you enjoyed reading False Flag please do consider leaving a review on the platform you purchased it. Not only do reviews help and support me write more books they are also essential for acceptance to book promotion programmes that help me find new readers.

You can also support me to become a full time writer by **supporting me at Patreon**. Patreon is a platform that enables patrons to help creatives fulfil their true potential.

Thanks again,
Jay Tinsiano

False flag (or black flag) describes covert military or paramilitary operations designed to deceive in such a way that the operations appear as though they are being carried out by other entities, groups or nations than those who actually planned and executed them.
  Wikipedia

PROLOGUE

1991

Chiu Wah On smiled at his old friend; metallic black, compact and powerful. He felt the weight of the SIG Sauer P225 Pistol in his coarse hands and checked the recoil actions to ensure everything would work perfectly.

Lighting a cigarette, Chiu inhaled and blew out grey smoke that wafted upwards, dispersing against the whirring ceiling fan. His fingers ran over the long scar that went from his forehead and around his left cheekbone; a constant reminder of that bloody night, before settling on the solid form of the weapon again.

Chiu knew the weapon inside out, as if it were an extension of his body, and had handled it many times in training. It was a widely used handgun and not easy to trace or be attributed to any particular source.

The first time he had fired the pistol felt like it was only yesterday. The execution yard in Nanjing, capital of Jiangsu province, under a stark, grey sky. Two People's Liberation Army guards escorted a shackled prisoner into the empty concrete yard, pulling off his cloth hood to reveal the broken face of a man aged around twenty, eyes wet with tears as they settled on Chiu in anguish.

His superior handed Chiu the loaded P225 and gave him a level stare. He took it and looked into the eyes of the prisoner for a moment, before swiftly raising his arm and firing point blank into the forehead. Every detail, every sound, was crisp in his mind. The shot, followed by the slump of the body on the hard concrete ground, and finally the words of praise from his superior. His first live kill gave Chiu a grim satisfaction, enabling him to move on from years of raw frustration.

The cheap Bangkok hotel room was low lit. Net curtains across the open window wafted in the breeze and the walls faded into a sickly brown from years of stale cigarette smoke. A television flickered silently in the corner and the occasional roar of a moped or tuk-tuk filled the room. He had not left the hotel for three days now and it felt like the walls were closing in on him. Thankfully, the killing would soon begin.

Chiu wrapped the pistol and cache of bullets in a cloth, tucked them into a red canvas bag and then placed it back into the bottom of the wardrobe. Patience, he kept telling himself, over and over. Patience.

CHAPTER 1

Two months earlier

A strong wind swept the rain across the dual carriageway and through the valley where Frank Bowen had killed time in his teens. There would soon be dozens of red brick houses built and he wanted to hold and embed that place in his memory before it changed forever. There was something comforting to him about the trash and old car tyres lying abandoned on the unused road.

"Here, boy!" Frank whistled to Scotty, who was sniffing around the ground and ignoring him, as he followed a scent trail. He was Jodie's pet, but walking him made for a great excuse to get away from the flat.

Thick droplets of rain began to build and then within seconds, it came down as a torrent. A nearby derelict car garage offered shelter and Frank ran inside. The windows were now broken black holes that had not seen occupants for over a decade.

Further up the hill, the last solitary houses stood on the rain-washed road set against the grey shapes of two North London tower blocks. He had heard the developers were waiting for the owners to either move or die, so they could get on with their big project.

He considered going to look at the old house where he'd grown up with his parents before the accident, but the rain was coming down harder and it was getting late.

Scotty, bored with being soaked, finally scurried over to join Frank in the dry and shook himself off, spraying his trousers.

"Thanks for that," Frank sighed. As the terrier investigated the inner corners of the garage, Frank stared out at the relentless downpour. The rain always had a therapeutic effect on him, almost like a comfort blanket for the soul.

Scotty came trotting back and looked up at Frank in anticipation. "Want to go home now?" The dog merely looked up at Frank, his tail wagging excitedly.

"Great. Let's get out of here."

******

The following morning the skies remained threatening as Frank jogged along the docks past the endless offices and suits making their way to work. His dark hair and heavy set appearance made him look older than his twenty-six years. A fact not lost on him when he was younger and looking to get served in the pubs. An old man in combats and a tweed jacket tossed pieces of bread to a group of swans in the water. They rushed at the surprise snacks, beaks pecking gratefully.

A sudden screeching noise pierced the peaceful calm. A sickening crash followed by painful screaming came from the main road that ran parallel to the docks. Frank slowed his jog down to a walk and moved towards the commotion. A man in his mid-twenties was lying on the cobbled street, his body contorted– along with his mountain bike – under a car. Several pedestrians stopped and gawped; some continued to walk by.

"Quick! Somebody! Get an ambulance!"

A woman had already jumped out of the driver's seat, her hands on her head as she took in the scene in front of her.

"Oh Jesus, I didn't see..."

A burly man in a grey suit stood transfixed as dark blood soaked the dusty, cobbled road. Frank knelt over the man, trying to comfort him, impossible though it was—his face white and contorted, shrill screams and moans, short quick gasps for breath, eyes wide with fear. Eyes that were transfixed onto Frank's.

"It's ok, mate ... what's your name? It's ok. An ambulance will be here soon." Frank turned to the crowd: "Has someone called a bloody ambulance?" He looked back at the man on the ground, eyes frozen, staring skywards.

"On its way!" shouted a voice. The driver of the car was weeping and being comforted by another cyclist. After an agonising wait, the ambulance eventually pulled up, quickly followed by other emergency services. A paramedic rushed over and immediately felt his pulse and for any sign of a heartbeat, but the young man's life was already over.

****

Frank put down the keys on the kitchen bar and glanced at a pile of letters on the sideboard.

Jodie came in with a quizzical look from the living room where a home decoration programme blared out, exclaiming the delights of living room renovation.

"Hi, Frank. There's some post for you."

"Yeah I saw, thanks," he said, ignoring the letters. "How was your day?"

"Oh you know, the usual. The excitement never starts," she smiled at him thinly. "So, you're home early?"

"Yeah. I skipped work after what I saw going in. Some poor guy got killed. A cyclist was hit by a car."

Jodie's face turned to shock.

"Oh God!"

"It was nasty, horrible. He really suffered. I don't think he was much older than me."

Jodie rubbed Frank's arm in a rare show of affection. They embraced, her hands moving around him tentatively, as she patted his back. Frank bristled. She had been doing that a lot lately. He recently read in a body language book that it was a subconscious sign the person was not entirely comfortable with what they were doing.

"Makes you think doesn't it?" he whispered.

She pulled away from him and tilted her head. "About what?"

Frank moved to the kitchen bar and grabbed an apple from the fruit bowl.

"Life ... and its rich tapestry. It's so bloody short."

Jodie rolled her eyes.

"How many times have we had this conversation? I know you lost your parents, Frank, and then your grandad. I know how hard it's been for you. I just don't know what to say anymore."

"What? I didn't say anything about my parents or grandad."

"But that's what you meant! And what about me? What about us and a family?"

"What about..? Jodie, I've just seen a guy, lying in his own blood, die in front of me!"

The dog barked and disappeared into the living room.

"Don't shout in front of Scotty."

Frank shook his head while Jodie glared at him and snatched her keys off the kitchen bar.

"I'm taking him for a walk. Away from you." The door slammed.

The death of Frank's grandfather, Larry Bowen, a few months earlier had put a hold on the bickering, but now a return to past form seemed to be back on the agenda.

Frank took a bite from the apple and flicked through the letters. He didn't recognise one as a bill and opened it. It was from his grandfather's solicitor, entitled 'Inheritance'.

He read the words slowly. It told him how he had inherited five thousand pounds from his grandfather's estate. There was just the matter of signing a few forms at his convenience.

Five grand. It was a nice rounded amount, not life-changing, but handy nevertheless. He had expected to receive something but had no idea how much it was going to be. Larry Bowen had always scrimped and saved, despite not earning a great deal.

Frank did a quick calculation. He had around three or four thousand pounds of debt to pay off from the inheritance, which, on any other day would have irritated him. Today, however, he had seen a young man die and that experience had put all into perspective.

He carefully folded up the letter, went to the bedroom and placed it inside a book that lay on his bedside cabinet and then sat on the bed, staring at the wall.

The eyes of the young cyclist stared back at him as his life ebbed away. Frank supposed that at least someone had been there to comfort him at the end. Snuffed out, just like that. Going to work one minute and then...bang! Game over. It was life, but it was no easier to comprehend.

Then a thought came to him and he went to the wardrobe and took out a cardboard box. Inside was an assortment of his grandad's possessions, including letters, photographs, a watch and a leather-bound book. Frank hadn't really looked through all this stuff before and browsed through the items.

The images offered a very brief snapshot of his grandfather's life. Larry as a young man in the boxing gym where he had been a keen fighter for a few years; Larry and his late wife, taken in the 1970s; Larry standing tall, with a group of other men, all proudly posing in their British army uniforms, smiling broadly at the camera—handwritten on the back in faded blue ink, read: 2nd Infantry Division June 1945.

Then Frank noticed one of his parents that he hadn't seen before: young, happy, together. Frank found himself wondering what it would have been like if they had still been alive. Would he have taken them on a trip somewhere as they had aged? Visits on Sundays for a slap up roast, maybe? Helping his mum with the parsnips that she always forgot to do, even though they were his favourite ... listening to Dad moan about his beloved West Ham United. Yes, he would have done all that. No doubt about it, he would have been there for them.

Frank realised he was tightly gripping the photograph, tears escaping his eyes. He was recycling memories again, memories that didn't even exist. "What an idiot you are, Frank," he whispered out loud. He could not remember feeling more alone.

CHAPTER 2

The Waterfront bar, nestled on the Thames, bustled with the after work milieu of white-collar workers spilling their work gossip of bad bosses and good bosses. Frank spotted his friend, Carl at the quieter end, gazing over at the boats that lined the dockside. He caught his eye and gestured with his hand as to whether he wanted another drink. Carl gave the thumbs up.

"Alright, Carl?" Frank planted down the drinks and slipped into a chair.

"Great, thanks. So, Mr Bond, how's tricks?"

Both men clinked glasses. "I'm thinking of leaving Jodie, Carl."

Carl's face switched from a smile to shock in an instant. He stared at Frank, waiting for the punch line. None came. "Oh Shit."

Frank nodded grimly. "I know she doesn't love me anymore, Carl. And I'm seriously confused about how I feel, but one thing I do know; I'm not feeling good right now."

Carl exhaled slowly and stared at nothing in particular on the plastic tabletop.

"Sorry to hear that mate. That is a shocker," he said quietly.

He looked directly at Frank and added, "Most people who are unhappy can't bring themselves to make that decision. They hide from it. But we're only here once right? Anna and I are tight, but I'd be lying if I said we didn't have our ups and downs."

Frank sipped his pint and then looked out of the window at a couple strolling along the waterside. "I hear you. Part of me still wants it to work out, but I can't see how it will."

"How long have you been together?"

Frank sighed. "Four years, give or take."

Carl nodded silently and took a sip of his ale.

"Listen, Carl, I know you have a lock up garage. I wanted to stash some of my things for a while."

"Oh? Well, of course, you can. Going somewhere?"

"Yeah, to travel for a bit. I want to see some of this beautiful world before I pop my clogs. Also, I really should be getting some sun. This non-stop crap weather is getting me down."

Carl smiled. "I'll second that. Good for you. Whereabouts?"

"I'll start with Goa in India. Then go to Thailand and then see what comes up."

Carl gave a whistle, "Nice! I'm jealous. Just avoid the Middle East right now. There's definitely going to be a war kicking off over there."

"Oh right? Yes, I'd heard something about that. No chance of avoiding it then?" Frank hadn't bothered too much with the news recently. He had other things on his mind and, although he worked at a newspaper, his department dealt with advertising rather than the stories of the day.

Carl leaned forward and lowered his voice. "Not likely. Saddam could basically dance a jig and sing the Star-Spangled Banner; it wouldn't make a blind bit of difference. The Iraqi government somehow got the impression they had the green flag to invade Kuwait, but things have changed."

"Well you can't go around invading countries, no matter what," replied Frank.

"No, you certainly can't."

Frank manoeuvred the ashtray and sparked a cigarette. "So, how is life in MI6?"

"Busy. Between you and me, you ain't seen me, right?" Carl tapped his nose, winked and they both laughed. Carl had been an intelligence officer for six years and wasn't able to speak about any aspect of his job to anyone. It had never bothered Frank. In fact, he didn't want to know.

Frank took a large gulp of his Guinness and Carl looked serious again.

"I'm really sorry about Jodie. I'll help out any way I can. Just think of it as a new beginning, mate," assured Carl.

They clinked glasses. "A new beginning."

CHAPTER 3

The sleek black W126 S-Class Mercedes travelled north alongside the Temple of Earth Gardens in Beijing. Years before, Zhang had regularly visited with his parents, running along the tree-lined paths that cut through gardens. The walkways converged on the central altar, Fang Ze Tan, where Emperors of the Ming – and later Qing dynasties – had made sacrifices to appease the gods and help the nation.

It had been so long since he had visited any of the Temples, the others being the Temple of the Sun and the Temple of the Moon, which had all played an important part in the city's history. Zhang considered taking a walk there later that afternoon if only to offer credence to the sacrifices he himself was about to offer to the nation.

The Mercedes turned east onto Hepingli North Street, along the north border of the Gardens and into a quiet residential road, coming to a stop outside a restaurant. Zhang ordered his driver to stay put and climbed out of the car, walking up the steps to the glass doors, above which red lanterns hung, glowing in the dim light. He caught a reflection of himself in the glass – dark, swept back hair with his goatee beard, brown suit – and wondered if he would still be enjoying these privileges after the coming operation had played out.

The head waiter greeted Zhang as he came through the door and showed him into the empty restaurant, escorting him to his favourite table. He preferred it because it was near the window and more importantly, away from the ears of the kitchen. Three waitresses lined up to receive him, menus in hand; their uniforms immaculate, ironed and crisp. Zhang had earlier ordered the restaurant to be closed to the public.

The first waitress asked him what he would like.

"Green tea. With two cups. My associate will be here shortly. Also, please bring my Xiangqi board."

The waitress nodded and the three of them scuttled off as Zhang removed his jacket and placed it on the back of his chair.

A tall, gangly, middle-aged man in a dark suit entered and shooed away the head waiter as he walked across the carpeted floor, weaving between the empty tables. Zhang looked up and nodded as Peng Quan, his strategic advisor, hung his jacket over the spare chair and sat down, his sharp breaths suggesting he had been running.

"Peng, have you been working out?"

Peng raised his sharp eyebrows in confusion as he looked at his superior for illumination.

Zhang sighed as he bounced one end of his unlit cigarette on the table top. "Maybe you need some exercise. You're out of breath from walking from the car?"

Peng grinned sheepishly as he understood, "My driver parked down the road, I just jogged a bit. Sorry, I'm late."

The waitress returned with a tray holding a pot of green tea and two small china cups, decorated with gold patterns, and placed it on the table. She arranged the cups in front of the men and poured tea into each one. Zhang nodded his thanks and a second waitress appeared, holding a wooden box.

Zhang took it and placed it to his side, opening the lid to reveal the board and game pieces within.

"Thank you. That is all. Please do not disturb us."

The girl nodded and immediately disappeared.

Zhang opened the box and took out the lined game board and placed it in the middle of the table. He then carefully counted out the disked pieces that were engraved with a combination of red or black Chinese characters. The game, also known as Chinese Chess, was a popular strategy board game representing a battle between two armies and the object was to capture the General. In the middle of the board, a gap represented a river between the two opposing sides.

"I hope I can beat you this time, Peng," Zhang smiled broadly. "But then, on the other hand, beating my best strategic advisor might not be a good omen."

Peng laughed, taking his first sip of green tea. "We shall see, Ho Zhang."

Zhang had worked with Peng Quan for over twelve years in the intelligence community and he was the first person he requested for his small team when setting up the fifth department—a department that did not exist in any official documents or paperwork.

The Chinese apparatus consisted of four main bureaus: the General Staff Department that included organised sub-departments for artillery, engineering, armoured units, operations, training and a host of others, through to the Second Department for military intelligence. The Third was for monitoring of foreign armies and, finally, the Fourth that held the electronic intelligence portfolio, responsible for electronic countermeasures.

It had been Zhang's idea to form an elite unit specifically for 'off the record' black operations. The Fifth's agenda was to enhance and forward China's overseas influence without leaving footprints and, wherever possible, leave false trails to foreign agencies.

Zhang believed this was perfectly in keeping with the ministries' charge by the General-Secretary. That was to ensure "the security of the state through effective measures against enemy agents, spies, and counter-revolutionary activities designed to sabotage or overthrow China's socialist system."

The risk, however, was significant and the buck was always going to stop at Zhang. Such were the sensitive circumstances of the bureau's role, that there had even been a serious discussion about making it financially self-sufficient, even if that meant illegal activities like drug trafficking. Zhang was relieved when this idea was thrown out as it would have, no doubt, given him a myriad of headaches. He would rather leave that type of business to their Triad friends.

Peng Quan moved one of his soldier pieces forward one square, to start the game.

"We need to make a decision on our other game plan," said Zhang as he studied the board and moved one of his own soldiers.

"Yes, yes, I know," Quan replied.

"There are still two pieces missing," Zhang continued.

"Everything else has been set up and is ready to go," said Quan, his voice flat as if Zhang was chastising him. He moved another soldier forward on the board.

Zhang already knew this, having spent over two years involved in the planning. Every detail of the operation had been scrutinised and approved by him and yet there were still vital cogs that needed to be put in place. He scanned the board of play; wondering how he could get his cannon to control the middle of the board as soon as possible. He moved his piece, took a sip of tea and rested his eyes on the man opposite him.

"Without those two players, the game cannot commence and now is the time, Peng. All eyes are on the Gulf."

Quan advanced his horse on the same flank to counter Zhang's cannon.

"Has agent Bashe come up with anyone?"

"Not yet, but I'm hoping he will." As he spoke, Zhang's eyes moved over his opponent's pieces on the far side of the river, which was represented by the middle of the board, trying to second guess him. He moved a soldier piece forward onto Quan's side of the river.

"What about Orchid? Anything new come through?" Quan asked, casually, as he deployed one of his chariots one square forward. Zhang's eyes narrowed. He figured Quan must be looking to get it into his left corner, ready to threaten his general—a possible déjà vu of a previous game, where a 'Jiang si le,' checkmate had occurred almost before the game had begun. He contemplated moving his right advisor diagonally for a moment as he lit another cigarette, inhaling and slowly blowing out a plume of grey smoke that snaked up to the high, dark red ceiling.

"No, Orchid is standing by and will be called upon. You did a good job recruiting our flower over there, by the way. They have been a great help working to an arrangement with our Triad friends for the handover." Zhang moved his right advisor disk.

"Thanks," Quan replied, but he was frowning at the board. He moved a long arm across the game of play and captured one of Zhang's soldier pieces.

Zhang smiled and considered a move that would surely involve the sacrifice of his castle but could enable him to push his Cannon up his opponent's right flank.

Sacrifices were always needed in war, he mused.

CHAPTER 4

Flight BA377 touched down at Goa airport at 4.20pm local time. Frank strained to see what he could out of the small window but gave up. The man next to him was just too large and had obscured his view for the whole journey. Reflecting on the difficult and emotional past few weeks Frank still wasn't sure if he was doing the right thing.

Moving all his remaining possessions into storage and saying goodbye to Jodie after four years together was a sad time and their parting had been far from amicable.

Maybe he deserved every scream and shout that had been directed at him, followed by the tears. She had looked forward to some kind of future between them and being five years older had anticipated having a family with him. At twenty-six Frank just felt he was too young. There were things he wanted to do with his life. Experiences to be had. Maybe someday he'd be ready for kids but not yet. Jodie had screamed that he was refusing to grow up. Maybe he wasn't ready to grow up. Had she considered that?

Frank felt drained and tired, mixed with a rising sense of excitement as he stared out at the deep blue sky through the windows opposite. He had been yearning to do this for so long. Every time he had walked past a travel agent, with their posters of beaches in paradise, he had stopped in his tracks and stared longingly at the flight prices.

The heat hit Frank like a wall as he stepped off the Boeing 757 and he immediately broke into a sweat. The air-conditioned arrivals hall provided some relief as well as a scene of chaos, as hordes of passengers stumbled around looking for their salvation. An Indian soldier chatted to customs officers, his weapon slung over his shoulder, plastic and shiny. The uniform he wore had a newly pressed and ironed look, reminding Frank of a life-sized action man.

His first destination was Anjuna beach. According to his hastily purchased travel book, it was a vibrant place to start. The plan was to find a beach and settle in for a month or so of relaxation and fun. Frank felt he deserved it. After all, he had been working non-stop for the last few years and it had felt like a hard slog. Pleasant in parts, but ultimately a humdrum period of his life.

As he stepped out of the airport doors, a posse of Indians, holding up pictures of their rental houses, swamped him and the other travellers. He felt like a monkey in the zoo and waved them away.

"No huts, thanks. I want a taxi."

A small, skinny Indian man grinned at Frank with yellow teeth, "I have great bungalow, cheap prices."

"No bungalows, thank you." The man nodded his head from side to side. "OK, mister. Taxi is no problem; I have one just up there."

Frank followed him across the dusty road to an old yellow Bristol car from the bygone British Empire. People were bustled into other vehicles, which kicked up clouds of dust as they drove off. Frank bundled into the back of the vehicle with three other travellers whom the driver had rounded up. He nodded a greeting to them.

"Where you from, mate?" asked a shabby haired, blond Australian man in the middle of the back seat. On the other side of the Aussie was a smart looking woman with a pierced nose. Her long, blonde, curly hair was pulled back into a ponytail; her face was soft and understated, yet classically beautiful. She turned and smiled at Frank.

"Just in from England; same as him," Frank gestured to the large man who'd been next to him on the flight, now welded into the front seat. He tried to turn around to acknowledge Frank for the first time, but couldn't quite manage it and gave up. The car occupants made small talk as the driver drove like a man possessed, swerving around potholes in the road, sometimes failing to avoid them at all. An occasional bump and shudder caused the passengers to grab onto anything remotely stable as they sped past Portuguese-style villas lining the roads.

Everyone in the car smiled despite the concern in their eyes and tried to talk over the noise. At last, the journey ended and Frank left the others to find a quiet spot, eventually finding what he wanted. It was a small beach house, set away from the crowded drop off point, yet close enough to the bars that adorned the beachfront.

He dumped his gear and immediately ventured out to his new surroundings. The air was sweet with the scent of jasmine and the deep blue sky opened up endlessly overhead. Closer to the beach, sun-kissed travellers milled around the bars, taking in the late afternoon sun and generally hanging out. There were characters that looked like they had been here for years, encrusted with the elements and destined never to leave. Everyone seemed to have beads hanging around their necks, sporting heavy tans, their movements slow in the heat.

An old Indian man in bright red football shorts played some kind of instrument that sounded like bagpipes and was paid to move on by a couple of sunbathing women. Dogs ran around wild, scavenging for food, and were consistently waved away.

Frank clocked a lively bamboo hub of activity called 'The Brazil Bar' and mooched up the wooden steps. Dub beats boomed from the stereo, spilling onto the beach. He ordered food and beer before sitting down to take in the scene.

"Hey, how's it going?" an American voice interrupted his thoughts. A young guy with shoulder-length blond hair sat down, uninvited, and slurped his Kingfisher beer.

"I'm good, just came in today," Frank said.

"Yeah, I thought so. You look a bit pasty if you don't mind me saying. You'll love it here though, this place really rocks. I've been here for two months. I was supposed to be headed to Thailand but haven't managed to leave here just yet," he gave Frank a broad smile.

"I could think of worse places to get stuck."

The American saw someone he knew and called over: "Theo, hey! Over here!"

A tall, middle-aged, Indo-Chinese figure moved over towards them, dressed in a white, short sleeve shirt, slacks and leather sandals, his jet-black hair tied back into a ponytail, eyes razor sharp, blue and piercing. He made for an impressive figure. Frank shook hands with him.

"Hi, I'm Frank."

"Theo." The man fixed Frank with a direct look and smiled warmly.

The American grinned. "Yeah, I'm Claude by the way." He shook hands with Frank as well, almost as an afterthought.

Theo talked slowly and deliberately, in direct contrast to Claude who seemed to race through his lines, as if speaking through a panicky oral exam.

"Here in Goa, life is about enjoying yourself and nothing else. You leave your worries at home and that's it."

Theo rolled up a joint as he spoke; piecing the papers together like it was the most natural thing in the world. Frank thought his accent was a strange mix of mid-Atlantic, but more British than American, and he reminded him of a Colombian villain from a T.V. series.

"If there is anything you want, I can get it for you. But be careful of the Takkas; the cops. They usually dress in plain clothes, but you will see them a mile off. You will learn this. I know some of them, so if you get into trouble, let me know."

"Good guy to know, huh?" Claude thumbed towards Theo.

Frank nodded, "Great. I'm not planning to get into any trouble though."

After a few minutes, Claude left to chat to a couple of women on another table and Frank talked with Theo for an hour or so. Theo told him he had been the only son of a Vietnamese mother and an Indian father. He hadn't settled and took off at every opportunity, travelling widely in Asia, but he had not yet visited any Western countries.

They touched on their lives and aspirations and Frank decided he liked Theo. He had a calm demeanour about him as if he regretted nothing and rolled with life like a leaf on a wave.

Frank decided not to go wild that night and hit the sack about ten.

Early the next morning, he awoke to the sun beaming in through the window blinds. It felt fantastic to smell the first morning abroad. Frank found a place to get breakfast and then walked along the beach towards a quieter part and sat watching the waves crashing onto the golden shore for a while. He wondered why he had never appreciated it like this before on all those trips to the seaside in England.

England. It seemed a million miles away now and a new life beckoned.

A figure approached from the market end of the beach, stopping occasionally to gaze out to the blue horizon. Frank watched the figure move closer and realised it was a woman dressed in an Indian style one piece dress. She stared toward Frank and he saw it was the curly haired blonde woman from the taxi. They hadn't really communicated in the cab, due to the Australian dude stuck between them.

She waved and walked over to Frank.

"Hello there. How are you finding it so far?' she smiled, her hand playing with a seashell. Frank noticed she had a necklace around her neck made from small coloured stones and sported a native look of a red dot on her forehead, just above the middle of her eyebrows. The third eye.

"So far, so good!" Frank gestured to her to sit down. "I'm just enjoying the sea," he said.

"It's beautiful, I love watching it," she agreed, parking in the sand next to him and brushing back her hair. Frank immediately noticed a delicate grace about her, as he had the day before.

"It's very therapeutic. It concentrates the mind," Frank said.

"A lot of the beauty is spoilt throughout India though. There's crap dumped everywhere. People have no idea what they're doing to the environment."

She gestured towards a mound of plastic bottles that had congregated nearby. "This is exactly what I'm talking about," she said, with contempt.

"Yeah, that is pretty bad. People are just here to party I guess. I'm Frank by the way," he held out his hand.

"Nice to meet you, Frank. I'm Maria."

They gazed out to sea and he noticed her painted toenails and jewellery. It suited her well, Frank thought.

"You've travelled around India quite a bit then?" he asked.

"Yes, I love it. I flew to Mumbai and went to Matheran and the Sahyadri hills. It's much cooler there and a really great place to relax. Then I came down to Goa on the train."

"That sounds great. I'm going to stay here for a while, and then I plan to move onto Thailand."

"Yes, I have to go there at some point, I won't stay long. I'd like to go to Indonesia then back to Hong Kong," Maria said.

"You live in Hong Kong?"

"My Father is based there. He's English and works for the Legislative Council of Hong Kong. They're all very busy preparing for the 1997 handover to China at the moment. Although it's still six years away you wouldn't believe the panic behind the scenes."

"Oh? What's going on?" Frank was intrigued.

Maria momentarily held her hands above her eyes to shield them from a glare of sunlight as she looked at him.

"Well, you remember the killings on Tiananmen Square a few years ago?" He nodded. The footage of the student standing in front of a line of tanks had become a powerful iconic image the world over. "It certainly hasn't helped put minds at rest," she said. "Then there's the power struggles as groups jostle for position. I also heard the triad gangs have done a deal with Beijing not to interfere."

"Hmm, really? Yes, there's probably a lot at stake," he said.

She gave him a broad smile. "I hear all about it from my Dad. All the, what's the English word? Gossip? I hear it all."

She looked serious again. "But there are a lot of worried people in Hong Kong right now."

"Do you think there'll be trouble?" he asked.

She leaned back; her elbows wedged into the sand and narrowed her eyes at a distant ship on the horizon. Frank couldn't help but cast his eyes over the contours of her body. She was beautiful and clearly relaxing into a favourite topic of hers.

"When there are governments fighting over land, with their agencies of limitless power, there's bound to be trouble."

CHAPTER 5

Pulsating beats drifted across the beach and a cyclone of colourful rays belted out over the top of the dancing masses as the moon winked over the calm night waters behind them. Frank spotted Theo through the crowd and moved towards him.

Theo turned and grinned. "Hey Franky; you enjoy?"

"Fantastic! Happy as Larry."

"Larry?"

"Oh! It's just an English saying," explained Frank.

Theo laughed and scanned his eyes through the dancing party-goers. "Hey, check out the beautiful girls over there!"

"There's way too many for me, mate," Frank said, smiling at Theo in the dim light.

Frank looked around for Maria but she had disappeared. After meeting on the beach they had walked to the flea market; a busy scene with snake charmers and old travellers flogging their junk. Then they had enjoyed some dinner together, some of the best fish Frank had ever tasted, before joining the beach party.

Theo motioned for him to move towards the edge of the crowd. Frank felt a cold sweat, his shirt sticking to his back. Theo began building a joint, but Frank suddenly craved water as he slowly became aware of his heart pumping hard.

"I'm going to find a toilet, Theo. I'll catch you later."

"Sure, Frank. See you later."

After pushing through the heaving mass, Frank eventually found a vacant toilet at the back of a bar and, on returning, pondered whether to stick around or call it a night.

"Hey!"

He turned to see a scowling, stooped, man leaning heavily on the bar. His white hair straggled around his bony brown neck and shoulders which held a bunch of necklaces, adorned with shells and what looked like bone fragments.

"They call me the dawg!" he growled at no one in particular. It sounded to Frank like his voice was scarred by a forty a day habit and penchant for whiskey chasers. The man then peered at Frank from under bushy, untamed eyebrows.

"How's it going, Dog?" Frank extended his hand for the Dog to shake, but he just stood staring over his shoulder at something behind him before walking off without another word. Frank shook his head in disbelief and turned around to be faced with a tall, blond, German man.

"Zat dog," he stated," is a legend around here!"

"I can tell he is," Frank said, sarcastically, wearily moving away to the exit, suddenly deciding he would call it a night after all. He strolled along the path amongst the palm trees and huts and as he glanced toward the trees near the parallel road, noticed Maria walking along a path that converged with his.

"Hey, Maria."

She turned her head at the sound of his voice. "Hey, Frank." Even in the limited light, he could make out her full beautiful smile.

"Did you have a good time? I lost you."

"Yes, it was busy. I went for a wander along the beach, and then went back, but I couldn't see you," she said.

They strolled through the moonlit palms. The beams from the beach party behind them continued to streak across their path like a myriad of beacons.

"Were you looking for answers in that view of the sea again?" he quipped.

Maria laughed, her hands still toying with a seashell, perhaps the same one she had earlier. "Yes, I didn't find many there though. It was much too dark to see anything."

They arrived at Frank's hut. "This is my grand abode," he said, catching her eye in the faint light before moving closer. He reached a hand to caress her cheek and their lips met hastily. Maria opened up to him, while Frank's hand moved around her waist, pulling her into him until her breasts pressed against him.

They moved inside the small hut and into the bedroom. Frank scrambled around for his lighter and lit his oil lamp, regretting his decision to go for a cheap hut without electricity. Maria took off her long, Indian style gown and unclipped her bra as Frank opened the mosquito net.

"Quick! Hop in!" he urged, smiling at her as he removed his shirt and shorts before diving in behind the safety of the net.

"I wouldn't want to share you with any mosquitoes," he whispered.

Frank felt her heart beat against his chest. Her skin felt smooth and warm against his and he welcomed it. She smelled sweet and it reminded him of something; a smell from the distant past.

****

An hour later, Frank ran his hand over Maria's slender curves as she lay on her stomach with her face turned towards him. He moved his hand up the small of her back to where the end of her curly hair lay easily on her skin. She looked at him with half-closed eyes; her face and mouth obscured by her arm, and let out a satisfied sigh. The flickering oil lamp danced animated shadows across their bodies and seemed comforting to Frank somehow, like the rain that transfixed him back home.

"What are you looking for out here?" she asked softly.

"Sun, sea and Dutch women," he said, with a cheeky grin.

Maria laughed. "I see."

Frank returned his gaze to her soft skin, listening to the sound of the lapping tide just outside the hut that seemed to draw closer as if closing in around their feet.

"I had a major urge to take off and leave. I broke up with someone. We didn't want the same things," said Frank.

"People drift apart every day, in the same way, they're pulled together," she said and slowly moved her hand over his chest. "Was it a long relationship?"

"A few years. We were supposed to get married. Kids; the works," Frank said.

"A pretty serious relationship then?"

"Oh yes. It was serious," he whispered, almost mockingly.

Frank turned his body towards her. "What about you? Any Dutch hunks waiting for you at home?"

Maria expelled a loud laugh.

"No, no. Not in Holland. I had a boyfriend in Hong Kong for a while. Nothing came of it."

"Chinese?"

"No. A Frenchman."

"A Frenchman in Hong Kong. Sounds like a novel."

"My life has been a bit of a novel, you could say," she said with a wry smile.

"I look forward to hearing all about it," said Frank, reaching for a cigarette.

"Any other family?"

Frank quietly sighed, wondering whether he wanted to continue this conversation. Usually, he didn't, when asked. He'd just lie or make something up, anything to avoid going down that road.

"No, unfortunately, they've all gone. My parents were killed in a car crash when I was seven. My only surviving relatives were my grandfather and Uncle. Grandad passed away a few months ago."

Maria turned onto her side, looking at him with genuine sadness, "I'm sorry Frank. That's awful. It must have been extremely hard for you."

Frank watched the spiral curl of bluish smoke waft up through the mosquito net.

"The pain recedes over time, but it never goes away. I do miss them, I really do. But I was so young. The memories of them are," he paused. "Kind of faded, you know?"

Frank stubbed out his cigarette and placed the ashtray outside the net.

They lay in silence for a while. The light gush of the tide seemed to slow down and sleep took them quickly.

****

Lightning forked across the black sky overhead, a power of nature that Frank had never seen before. It lit up the endless flat fields that surrounded their cottage for miles. He could even see the trees by the farm where he played army with his friends. There was a tree house there, where they kept their plastic toy guns. The endless dykes acted like trenches and in a field next to the farm stood unused tractors that had been left to rust for years.

She held his hand tight.

"It's OK sweetheart. It's just a storm."

They waited for Dad on the cottage doorstep, clutching their coats as protection against the downpour.

"Come on, Patrick, we're late," his mother shouted.

Frank's father appeared behind them, his anorak rustling as he sorted through his keys. "Right, get ready and make a run for it," he said.

The three figures sprinted down the pathway to the Ford Escort parked on the road and they all clambered inside as quickly as they could.

Patrick turned to his son in the back seat. "You all belted up, Frankie boy?"

"Yes, Dad."

"Good lad."

Patrick started the engine and the windscreen wipers kicked into action, barely keeping the torrent of rain at bay.

"God, would you look at that?" His mother stared across at the field opposite the house.

Patrick and Frank followed her stare and saw the cow, lying on its back with one hind leg stuck upwards as straight as a pole. The carcass looked frozen as if it had been struck by a spear from the sky.

"What happened to it, Dad?"

"It must have been hit by lightning. In the wrong place, at the wrong time. Poor cow," he said and laughed.

The car slowly moved off, momentarily getting closer to the strange sight in the field as they drove by. Frank's small face stared out of the window at the dead animal, and then he looked away.

CHAPTER 6

Frank opened his eyes with a shudder, breathing heavily, his body covered in a sheen of sweat. As the sound of his heartbeat inside his head receded, the familiar cricket noises and distant voices of early morning beach wanderers took over.

He turned to find Maria had gone and felt a pang of disappointment in his stomach. Something he said? Probably gone for a swim or breakfast, he thought, as he watched specs of dust float against slithers of light that beamed through the hut slats.

Eventually, he climbed out of bed, grabbing his wash bag and towel and padded out to the shower area; another perk of cheap boarding. The cool water rushing over his aching head felt like heaven and he let it stream down his body, eyes closed as he relished the feeling. He reached for his wash bag and fumbled around inside for the shower gel. A piece of paper fluttered down onto the concrete slab, narrowly missing the puddle of water that circled around his feet and landed on the hard, sandy ground.

Frank picked it up with one still dry hand and looked at it quizzically. It was written in neat, perfectly formed handwriting.

Thanks for a perfect night. If you're ever in Hong Kong:
(344) 37484 44
Maria x

Frank could only wonder why she had left him the message in his wash-bag. She had obviously decided to move on to her next destination but it seemed strange that she had left so quickly. Had she felt like their night together had been a mistake?

Feeling slightly aggrieved he tucked the note back in the bag. It would have been nice to spend more time with her but he decided to just get on with having a good time.

****

Lazy days drifted into party nights, the alcohol and drugs all part of the routine and, like a kid in a sweet shop, Frank was there: taking it all on.

He'd catch breakfast around four in the afternoon—if he could stomach it—with the regulars at the Brazil bar, then soak up the last of the sun and drift aimlessly in the blue sea. After a brief relaxation, it was time for beers and cocktails. Theo, Claude and a regular motley crew played cards and backgammon, turning the bar into a kind of beach style scene from Casablanca. Party night was every night. There was rarely a night off.

The comedown was hard and swift. One afternoon as he lounged on a hammock the pain hit him in the stomach, tying it up in knots and spitting it out again. He crawled to the safety of his bed as the sickness took hold; tiredness beating him up with sticks, weighing him down, preventing movement.

His appetite completely vanished, mouth dried up like a prune and he spent too much time in the toilet, wishing he had an en-suite bathroom. The terrible nights blanketed him in darkness, shrouding him in their cruel shadow, like a mocking demon. In his fever, he promised to look after himself, quit smoking, bump the drink, and be healthy.

It seemed to Frank that you were at your weakest exactly when you felt invincible.

After a few days, Theo came to see Frank and was visibly shocked at his appearance.

"Bloody hell, Frank, you look terrible!"

"I feel terrible, Theo; I think I'm going to die," Frank groaned.

"I doubt it." Theo looked closely at Frank, narrowing his eyes as if reading his health meter.

"My friend is a doctor; I'll go get him."

"Anything. Can you get me some more bottled water? I'll give you money for the Doc." Frank tried to move across the room to get to his cash.

"Forget it, Frank. You lie down."

When the doctor arrived he had Frank popping the antibiotics in no time. After a long period of praying and puking, Frank began to slowly recover, almost to his former self.

It was time to move on to his next destination. Thailand had always been in his travel plans and he was suddenly keen to get there.

Frank made a vague arrangement to meet Theo in Bangkok. As they drank tea in the Brazil bar, Theo recommended a guesthouse near the Khao San Road and pointed to it on a map.

"It's a great place, good price and very comfortable."

"Great," said Frank. "It's good to know where to go, saves a lot of hassle."

Frank found himself thinking about Maria again and wondered where she had gone. He hoped she was still around Goa and that there would be a small chance they would bump into each other again. He wanted to hear her seductive Dutch accent one more time, but it was not to be.

CHAPTER 7

Mu Heng banged the top of the small television that sat in the corner of his desk, attempting to get the picture back. It had been steadily getting worse for the past few weeks and had finally died. He eventually gave up and switched it off; slumping back into his chair. Heng checked his watch: 2.37am.

Where the hell was the team?

Patience was not one of his better qualities and the waiting had been going on for months. This had to rank as one of the most boring cover jobs he had ever been assigned, although at least the booth was quiet, he supposed. It was the slow passage of time that got to him. Still, at least now the waiting would soon be over.

Tonight was the night it would finally start to happen.

He flipped through the Hong Kong Times and then lifting his stocky figure up, walked outside the booth and lit another cigarette. Heng then paced up and down on the shiny tiled floor of the Kennedy Town Mass Transit Railway station, brushing imaginary dust off his grey uniform.

The shrill ring of the phone punctured the silence and he quickly picked it up and heard a low, rasping voice.

"Package is here, waiting."

"OK! On my way," said Heng. He slammed down the phone, grabbed a bunch of keys, his walkie-talkie and then made his way out of the booth and along the platform in the stark, artificial light.

Heng slid the metal gate linking the platform to the exit tunnel aside, where three grim looking Chinese men, each carrying heavy duty holdall bags, stood waiting. The man in the middle – with the arched scar – nodded and, without a word, they followed Heng back across the platform towards the booth, their footsteps echoing behind them.

CHAPTER 8

Bangkok. Khao San Road.

The smell of fried chicken hit Frank's nostrils as he jumped from the taxi. The thick air seemed almost unbreathable. A Westerner grinned at him from a café table as if Frank were a patsy in a creampie joke. He shoved some baht notes at the driver, determined to find this guesthouse as soon as possible.

It took a while for Frank to get to the guesthouse that Theo had recommended. He almost considered going to the first place he saw, but then decided against it and soldiered on. Eventually, another English tourist pointed him in the right direction.

The room in the 'Sunny Beach' was clean; the ceiling fan provided cool comfort for half an hour as Frank smoked cigarettes and watched the propelling blades slice up the grey cloud. A high-pitched whine stung in his brain. Frank decided to lay off the alcohol for a while. Those drinks on the flight from India hadn't done him any favours.

The outside eating area was a small courtyard where he'd come through from the side street earlier and was decorated on all sides with beautiful mosaic tiling, featuring a Buddha dominating a Thai landscape. It was a quiet spot, well away from the frantic Khao San, and Frank felt relieved he'd followed Theo's advice.

He wanted a drink and a bowl of noodles, and then remembered he was off the booze, but when the waitress came over he decided to order a Singha beer anyway. Looking around at the clientele, Frank could see a few Thai office workers and old travellers killing time at the tables. An old, silver-haired, tanned guy in a red shirt read the Bangkok Post and smoked a cigar.

Another man stopped at his table. He had a young Dirk Bogarde look about him, with jet black hair, sideburns and a five o'clock shadow on his chin and wore typical English attire: long sleeved shirt and white slacks.

"Mind if I sit here?" he asked.

"Of course, no problem," said Frank.

"Just arrived?" the man enquired.

"Yeah, I came from Goa. I'm headed south as soon as I can get out of here."

They introduced each other as Frank's beer and Thai noodles arrived.

"I'm Richard."

"Frank."

Richard ordered himself a coffee.

"Bangkok is an extremely interesting city. It can be a tad daunting on first arrival though."

"It's manic. I've only been here a couple of hours but I'm not planning to hang around."

"Well, you can't leave until you've visited the infamous Pat Pong." Richard winked at him.

"Oh, what's that?" Frank asked, sucking in his noodles.

"You don't know about Pat Pong? It's girlie bar central, Frank. It's where the action is," said Richard. He noticed Frank didn't look convinced and added, "Don't worry, we'll just look around and have a laugh."

****

The tuk-tuks swarmed through the early evening traffic, weaving past helmetless bikers and Japanese cars. The pollution rose in the air like a mist, making the city's buildings look like grey husks through the taxi window. Golden roofs of little temples tucked away amongst the shanty huts, jutted into the dimming sky.

The two men paid the fare and joined the crowd that milled around two parallel roads of Pat Pong. It was packed with T-shirt stalls, girly bars and prostitutes of every manner. There was certainly a seedy feel about the place. Richard warned that it was easy to get ripped off, but he knew a good place to go.

They were constantly harassed by gangs of girls or Thai pimps. Frank glanced into a passing bar and caught a glimpse of a beautiful Thai girl, dressed in a bikini, gyrating around a silver pole. She was closely watched by a gaggle of men at the bar.

Richard turned to Frank, smiling, as they fought through the crowd and pointed towards a side street. "I was down here last week," he started saying as they negotiated the crowd. "I saw a group of Rugby lads fight their way out after they were asked for an extortionate amount of money for their beers."

They paused to let a group of singing young German men pass them by.

"Another time there was a chap who had to flee for his life from a strip bar," Richard continued, "he was chased by machete wielding Thais who ran the place."

"What did he do?" asked Frank.

"I heard later that he accidentally insulted one of them. And he groped one of the girls which obviously didn't go down well." They turned left into an alleyway.

Great, thought Frank, sarcastically, as Richard rang a doorbell to a sinister looking metal door. A slot zipped open for a moment before the sound of a bolt unlocking the door revealed an older Thai woman peering out from the darkness. She held a torch to their faces and Richard quickly gave her some money. The two men followed the torchlight along a blackened corridor which led up a series of steps. She knocked on another door and babbled something in Thai before it opened to a buzzing interior, tinged with red light.

A bar ran all the way around a raised stage where people hunched over their drink and watched a group of dancers swing their stuff. To the back of the dimly lit room lay further tables and seats on different levels. The two men took seats at the bar and ordered beers. A group of young Thai girls in bikinis immediately surrounded them.

"Buy a drink for lovely girl?"

"Wanna try nice girls like us?"

Frank smiled at them. "We're just here for the show and a beer."

"Beer shit. Try hot Thai girl," one of them said. Frank laughed, wondering how he had been persuaded to come here.

Richard ordered drinks for the girls, which consisted of an inch high measure of orange juice and cost the same as their beers. He gave them to the girls who made small talk before leaving them to find more willing customers. After a while, a young couple came on stage and started a live sex show for the crowd. Twenty or thirty positions later, they trooped off. Their bored expressions throughout the entire spectacle indicated it was just another day at the office. Frank took in the seedy atmosphere and drank the beer in quick gulps.

"There's a free table at the back, let's grab it," said Richard.

"You're a sad old man, Rich, knowing these type of places," Frank said jokily.

Richard laughed. "Yeah. Just red-blooded. But it's all part of Bangkok's rich tapestry, you know."

Richard gestured for more drinks from the waitress dressed as a Playboy bunny.

"I like to live a certain type of life, Frank." He lit his tenth cigarette of the hour. "I can meet people here. For the kind of business, I do."

Frank sensed a change of tone in the conversation.

"There are ways of staying out here and making money and that's what I do. I'm not a traveller Frank, I live here."

He smiled again, but Frank could tell by his eyes he wanted to get something off his chest.

"I guessed as much," said Frank. "So how does someone from the old country make a living here?"

"Well there are all kinds of business one could get into. Asians love to do business, Frank. It's in their blood. That's what I love about it over here. No bullshit."

"Yeah I can imagine," nodded Frank.

Richard continued to talk about the black market, currencies, precious metals like gold, even selling snakes. It was a crash course in being a hustler in Thailand. After a few more beers, Richard mentioned he had a problem. He needed someone to bring some gems to Bangkok from the south. It was an easy deal, easy money. No borders to cross. He used travellers all the time, apparently.

"Thanks for the offer, Richard, but it's not really my line. Not right now anyway," he said.

"No problem, Frank." He searched his wallet and gave Frank a business card that only had a Bangkok phone number on.

"Just give me a call if you change your mind."

Frank took the card and slipped it into his wallet.

CHAPTER 9

The night bus left Bangkok in the early evening, heading south. Frank's head felt like it was lagging a few feet behind him, due to the relentless drinking nights that Richard had persuaded him to go on. He exhaled in relief and was glad to be leaving the manic city behind him and fell into a deep sleep.

Around five o'clock the following morning the coach pulled into Surat Thani; the bright sunlight already bathing the streets in a yellow glow despite the early hour. Frank grabbed his bag and headed off to find out the boat times to Koh Samui. Scanning the timetable, Frank could make no sense of it and wandered over to a nearby café to ask the owner. A tall, burly, dark-haired man had the same idea and was turning back from talking to the small, jovial faced proprietor.

"There's a six-hour wait," he said to Frank's unasked question.

"For the boat to Samui?" Frank asked.

"Aye. You'd think they'd put 'em on more regular, like."

The big man slung his huge backpack down next to a table in a way which suggested he was going no further. Frank joined him for breakfast, ordering banana pancakes and coffee whilst the Irishman ordered half the menu. He offered his massive hand to Frank.

"Jimmy," he said, a smile forming across his broad, deep-set features. Jimmy was a bus driver from Lisburn, Northern Ireland. But driving buses was just one of a long list of occupations. He'd taken off two years previously and had been over the Americas and was now covering Asia. They drank bottles of rice whiskey to pass the time until finally their 'Coconut boat', a two-level transporter that crammed in as many travellers as possible, was available for the crossing.

Once they had both finally arrived on the island, the two men found a tuk-tuk and headed for a stretch of beach called Choeng Mon, which Jimmy had heard about. They found a bungalow each, behind the guesthouse restaurant but only metres from the beach. They did their own thing in the day and met up for meals in the guesthouse restaurant, Frank burning his mouth on Coconut Soup and Thai style curries, which he was developing a taste for, and Jimmy trying everything without hesitation. The menu was geared to tourist 'Farangs' and wasn't very adventurous, but Jimmy managed to persuade the waitress to deliver 'off the menu' real Thai food.

One balmy evening, after dinner, Frank took his leather waist bag with his money and passport to the reception to book a boat trip, while Jimmy decided to stretch his legs and walk up the beach. Then he spotted that the best hammock on the beach was free and decided to grab it.

Swinging lazily, Frank watched the sun disappear below the horizon amid magical colours of the emerald sea. Daydreaming of the next stop on his trip; he weighed up whether to head to Penang in Malaysia or to carry on down the coast of Thailand to Kota Bharu.

The light faded fast and Frank finally went to return his money bag to the guesthouse safe, but no one was around at reception. He walked back to his hut, stashed the bag in the bottom of his rucksack, locked the door and headed for the beach to see if he could catch up with Jimmy. A Thai man in black shirt and long shorts walked past him, avoiding his eye.

The beach became deserted once past the last busy bar that catered to a happy drunk crowd, apart from the sounds of the lapping sea. Pink and neon blue lights winked in the darkness ahead and Frank moved towards them, stumbling in the thick darkness. The lights turned out to be a small lonely bar and Frank made out a Thai woman serving a man. Getting closer, he recognised Jimmy's distinct Northern Irish accent.

"Hey Jimmy, had a good night?" Frank said as he patted him on the back and pulled up a stool.

"Hey, Frankie, how're ya doing there? This is Mimi," he gestured to the middle-aged woman, who gave Frank a broad smile.

Frank eased onto another stool and slapped his Lucky Strikes onto the bar top.

"Very nice to meet you, Mimi. I'll have what he's having."

Mimi grabbed a bottle from the cooler and put it in front of Frank with another beautiful smile before disappearing around the back.

"So, been in touch with anyone back home?" asked Frank, as he started to pull off the bottle label, bit by bit.

"Home? Yeah, haven't been back there for a while. To be honest, there are a lot of bad memories back there," Jimmy's huge forearms dominated the bar and he shrugged.

"Ahh, sorry to hear that, Jimmy. We're all running from something I guess."

"Well, my da' was killed in an I.R.A. bomb when I was fifteen or so. He was a policeman. It was a kick in the teeth for a lad to lose his father like that."

Frank shook his head. "I'm really sorry mate, I didn't realise. I lost my parents when I was young. Car crash."

Jimmy grimaced in sympathy and he held up his beer: "To loved ones." A clink of bottles. "Yes, let's drink to that."

The light began to break as the two men staggered through the sand. The orange glow of a rising sun sparkled on the sea, revealing a fishing boat out on the bay.

"This is the best thing I ever did, so it is," Jim started, admiring the same view Frank was.

"All those shitty days of packing, driving and shovelling crap in people's gardens. It's like, why doesn't everyone just take off, leave it all behind? This is what I'm gonna do from now on, Franky boy, jus' work when I can and travel and enjoy the world's beauty whenever possible."

"Exactly right," Frank agreed.

As they approached their line of huts in the early morning light, Frank noticed something was wrong. The towel he'd left hanging outside was strewn over the steps, his door was slightly ajar and, with a sinking feeling, he suddenly noticed the damage of a forced entry on the frame. Inside, his clothes were strewn over the floor. He dived down into his bag, desperately looking for his money and passport. Both were gone.

"Shit!"

"I'd better check my hut too," said Jimmy and he quickly moved across the yard.

Frank tried to retrace his steps in his alcohol-riddled mind.

Jim returned after a couple of minutes.

"My place too, only I left my valuables with the restaurant owners."

Frank stood up, looking around, flushed with anger. "Shit! I just cashed in a large travellers' check!" he punched the wooden wall suddenly, with the side of his fist, and stepped outside, looking around angrily, as if the culprit might just still be hanging around.

He slumped down on the steps to his bungalow, sobering up quickly as the realisation hit that he was now virtually penniless, apart from the small amount of money he had on him.

****

"Hi ... Richard?" There was a pause on the line.

"This is Richard."

"It's Frank, from Bangkok. We went to Pat Pong. Remember?"

"Oh yes, Frank. How are you? Enjoying the sights?"

"Yes, or I was. I have a little financial problem. I was thinking about your offer."

"I see. Sorry to hear that. Where are you now?"

"Well I'm at Suret Thani, I've just been to Koh Samuri."

"Can you go to Krabi? I have a friend there."

"No problem."

"Great. Find the 'Bird House' in Krabi town. It's very quiet down there. You'll meet a guy called Greg. Be there by the fifteenth; that gives you a week. He'll give you everything you need."

"Thanks. Listen, I've a friend in the same boat, we both got robbed at the same time. He's an Irish fella. Is there anything he could do? He's broke as well."

Richard exhaled slowly over the line.

"I'm not sure. Probably not right now, not this time, but we'll see ... maybe something later. What's his name?"

"It's Jimmy Duffy, but it's no problem, Rich. Thanks, mate."

"Goodbye, Frank." The line went dead.

CHAPTER 10

Theo left his rented condo overlooking the beach in a short-sleeved white shirt and slacks. A Toyota pick up truck stood outside, its engine purring as Theo climbed in. He nodded at the driver and they pulled away.

The Toyota moved fast down the Mapusa-Anjuna road towards the town of Mapusa inland.

"Take it easy," said Theo, in Chinese Mandarin.

The truck paused at a crossroads while a herd of goats were shepherded across, and Theo leaned and spat from the window. His mirrored sunglasses glinted against the hot sun, turning towards an old man who was sitting outside a makeshift wooden snack stop. His watery eyes glanced up at Theo briefly, considering him for a moment before looking away. He reminded Theo of photographs he had of his late father, Daaruk Kumar.

Daaruk had come from Southern India and had always wanted to help people throughout his life. Born in the Bengaluru region, he had moved to study at Mumbai University and made the decision to join the International Red Cross. The war in Vietnam had begun and Daaruk found himself based in Saigon at the Red Cross Vietnam Southern branch where he met Theo's mother, Pham Thi Qui, a Vietnamese nurse. Eighteen months later, Theo was born – as Amith Kumar – in 1968, just as the combined forces of the North Vietnamese Army and Viet Cong launched the Tet offensive against U.S. army positions.

Daaruk's work required him to be based up towards the war zone for a while, just as the war intensified. On a particularly humid hot day in May 1969, Daaruk and his small team entered a village to bring medical supplies. A passing U.S SeaCobra attack helicopter sweeping the area mistook them for Viet Cong and attacked them with machine gun fire. There were no survivors.

The young Amith and his mother weathered the storm until 1975 when Saigon fell to the Communists. The bitterness at his father's death stayed with Amith throughout his youth and he was won over by the communist cause, joining the party and becoming an active member.

At the age of twenty, Amith travelled to Hanoi in northern Vietnam and worked for the administration of the party. Being mixed race, Amith had to work extra hard to prove his loyalty, but he didn't care. His aim was to make a difference in the way he saw the world, his motivation was a kind of vengeance.

After a few months, Amith got an opportunity to visit the Hong Kong branch of the Chinese Communist Party with his boss, for a strengthening of ties between the two parties. Amith was amazed at the wealth he saw on display there but equally disturbed by the hidden poverty embedded in the urban concrete jungle that was shown to them by the local party leader, Hu Lam.

"See how Capitalism divides and pushes down the poor here. They never show you this side of Hong Kong, do they?"

Amith had seen his share of poverty but had to agree it didn't make any sense considering Hong Kong's high per capita wealth. He was then introduced to a tall man from Beijing called Peng Quan. Quan told him, due to his cultural background, he would be a useful asset to the mainland's cause. China was soon to take back Hong Kong from the British and there was a lot of preparation required. And so Amith's involvement with the 5th department of Ministry of State Security had begun.

The truck negotiated the swarms of tuk-tuks, beaten up cars and scooters as they entered the town. It was market day; stalls and traders peddled their wares selling everything from fresh fruits, vegetables and livestock to carved wooden monkeys and fake branded clothing. The main street thronged and heaved with a mass of locals and the odd traveller checking out the offers.

The truck turned off and parked up in a quiet street, scattering a group of street dogs.

"I'll call you in a few hours and you can take me to the airport," Theo said, jumping out of the truck. The driver nodded and drove off. Theo unlocked a door that led through a garment shop, nodding to the owner, who impassively sat staring out toward the front. He then proceeded to climb a creaky stairwell and unlocked another door to a sparsely furnished office. There was a single desk, a filing cabinet with a fan on top and a table with a few papers scattered across it. Theo switched the fan on and removed a painting on the wall which revealed a safe door. He dialled the combination and pulled out an M-125 Fialka electro-mechanical cypher machine, which was the size of a typewriter, and placed it on the desk.

Theo then plugged it into a socket in the wall and connected it to the phone line before typing in the words: *Frank Bowen.*

CHAPTER 11

Frank shuffled along the shore from the phone booth and headed to the bus station with his heavy bag in tow. He had decided to travel to Krabi early to check everything out.

Krabi was indeed a quiet town. The streets ran in squares across each other and there was a main road along the riverfront, which moored various tourist boats and a seafood restaurant. Small islands jutted out from the emerald water as reaching for the clear sky. Frank had heard 'James Bond Island' was around here where they had filmed 'Man with a Golden Gun', but that little excursion would have to wait.

Frank looked at the notes he had jotted down when speaking to Richard. They included the name of the place with a rough map. The guesthouse café had an array of photos of local beach places to stay. There was no sign or mention of this 'Bird Cage' place though?

"I want to go the Bird Cage, tomorrow?"

"Bird Cage?" said the jovial, moustached, Thai man. 'There is a place called the 'Bird *House*' just outside town."

"Ah right. Yes, that's probably it."

"Run by Mr Ron."

"Uh huh."

"Do you bird watch?" the proprietor asked, looking at Frank intently through his shades.

"Uh? ...oh yes ... sometimes."

The man babbled Thai at a bored looking kid playing the computer game in the corner of the café and then picked up the phone and spoke to Mr Ron. The bored kid strolled past Frank and got onto a scrambler bike, revving the engine impatiently.

"Yes, he take you there now," the café owner gestured for Frank to jump on the back.

They scooted up through the town and up a steep hill where the countryside began. He busted a left through an open cast iron gate hidden from the road and, suddenly, they had arrived. It turned out Frank could have easily walked there in ten minutes, but at least he now knew where it was. He offered the bored boy a ten baht note, but he just smiled and took off without a word, leaving Frank alone in the undergrowth.

Plants grew high in the small, secluded garden and the grass was badly in need of a trim. Small insects buzzed in the evening ambience. There was a scent of sweet flowers lingering in the air and an old rusty bike leant against a white building that ran parallel to the path. Here were the guest rooms, a line of eight doors and a toilet and shower area at the end. Frank walked past the bike and saw the man sitting on the patio through the gloom.

Mr Ron stood up from his chair, sporting a white linen suit, and greeted Frank. He was average height, but more western looking than most Thais. It was the prominent nose and chin that made him look like an Englishman.

"Hello," he said, slightly effeminately, "I am Mr Ron. Can I help you at all?"

He seemed surprised at having a visitor but was warm and friendly and spoke fluent English with barely a trace of an accent. Behind him, there was a wide wooden patio with a railing extended over, what seemed like a marshland. The panoramic view extended across the horizon, revealing long grass, palm trees and little shack huts dotted in the distance. Beyond the jungle overgrowth, mountains rose on the landscape; grey hazed mounds for their distance.

"I know it's out of season and everything, but I wondered if I could hire a room for a week. I prefer a quiet spot like this, to staying in the town," said Frank as he walked slowly over to the railing, gazing out at the view.

"It is indeed a beautiful spot,' the Thai man agreed, moving elegantly to what looked like a disused dusty counter at the side of the bar. He took a key from a hook that belonged to pigeonhole shelves and handed it to Frank.

"Somewhere for the birds to come; that's why we have bird watchers stay here," he said, smiling.

"Yes, I can imagine."

Frank paid for a week and, as Mr Ron began to walk away, the Thai turned back to face Frank. "There's a fridge behind the counter, help yourself. Just write down what you've had."

With that, Mr Ron disappeared on his bicycle down the path, moving awkwardly through the long grass.

Frank had a smoke on the patio and gazed at the view again. Did Mr Ron have a connection with Richard or this Greg character? He was supposed to meet Greg here in five days time, but right now the place was completely dead. There was no one else there at all.

He looked in the fridge and saw a couple of beers and some lemonade Sprites. The bottle tops were slightly rusted and, on closer inspection, all the drinks in the fridge were long out of date. Cardboard boxes filled with old newspapers lay neglected behind the counter. Opposite the bar were more boxes piled up and an old sofa that had definitely seen better days.

He then checked out the room, which seemed clean and in order, then looked in the toilet and showers. Dead leaves fluttered across the pale tiled floor and large cobwebs lurked in the corners. It didn't look like there had been any guests for some time.

Frank lay on his bed, watching the ceiling fan whip through its rotation, and felt his eyelids flicker as they became heavy.

****

As if it were a harbinger of the death to come, a black crow flew across the road ahead and perched on the dark tree that looked evil to Frank's eyes. The bird hopped along towards the end of a branch and then suddenly froze as if to watch them drive by.

"You're driving too fast, Patrick!"

"No, I'm bloody not. It's a dual carriageway, a 70 miles per hour limit..."

Frank pulled his coat tighter around him as if to blanket out the anxiety.

"It's still too fast, I don't like it!" his mother shouted from the passenger seat.

"Stop arguing, I hate it," Frank whined, his little fingers fidgeting uncontrollably. His father turned his head slightly to address Frank. "Sorry, Frankie. Your mother, she's..."

"Watch out for that bloody lorry. It hasn't seen..."

The memory dimmed; time slowed down, taking its toll; spinning and rushing forward into the blackness. And then only a boy's scream remained.

A light faded into the darkness, circling slowly and then the face of a concerned woman filled his vision. "Are you awake?"

A dull pain on the side of the head helped bring the face into sharp focus. A nurse, with brown friendly eyes, clicked the torch off and stared down intently, brown wisps of hair fell around the back of her ears.

"Can you speak?" she asked.

The boy coughed and mumbled something which the nurse could not hear. "Do you want something to drink?" The boy shook his head.

"Where's my mum and dad?" he asked before coughing again.

"Shhh. It's ok. You try and get some more sleep, now."

****

Frank opened his eyes, his mouth felt like sandpaper and there was a distinct buzzing in his head. He sat up slowly and decided to stroll down to Krabi town for a bite to eat as the contact was not due for a good four hours.

Draining his beer bottle in the empty bar, Frank looked at his watch, a fake Omega he had picked up in Bangkok. Finally, it was nearly time to meet his Greg character.

After a walk back up the hill from the town to sit on the veranda at the 'Bird House' and listening to the crickets, Frank watched the odd starling fly across the horizon. He did a batch of press ups to burn off some energy and then paced around the patio.

About an hour later, Greg arrived and shook Frank's hand. He was French, average height, with a dark ponytail and goatee beard. He wouldn't look out of place on the backpack circuit. They went to Frank's room and Greg gave Frank a pack of two hundred cigarettes.

"Thanks. And the gems?"

Greg looked at him quizzically for a moment and then smiled.

"They're in one of the packs."

"Gems, not drugs, right? That's what we agreed."

The man looked offended for a moment.

"You can check. Definitely not drugs."

"OK. So where do you want me to go?" asked Frank.

Greg moved to the bed and took out a map of Bangkok, laying it flat on the yellow sheets, and pointed to a street near the Bangkok railway station with a pen.

"There's a country and western bar called 'Texan Bill's'. Richard will meet you there and pay you. Get there for the eighteenth. Seven o'clock in the evening."

He folded up the map again and put it in his pocket. His eyes flicked around the spartan room as he held out his hand.

"That's all. It's a piece of cake. See you again, perhaps."

Greg left the room and Frank listened to the hum of his car disappear as he stared at the Lucky Strike cigarettes on the bed. He picked them up. They were shrink-wrapped in clear film as if brand new.

The following day, Frank took the overnight tourist coach back to Bangkok. He hardly slept and his mind flipped between Jodie, his new friend Richard and then once again, Maria.

It was a strange way to say goodbye, disappearing like that. Still, she didn't owe him anything. It wasn't like they were an item. Frank couldn't help wondering if he'd see her again. There were so many faces while travelling, he thought, most of the time they turned up again somewhere along the trail.

Frank didn't intend to hang around Bangkok for long. He wanted to sort out a new passport from the Embassy to replace the stolen one and get his money.

Texan Bill's was a themed country and western bar, where the waitresses wore cowboy Stetson hats and a small band played bluegrass to the delight of what Frank assumed was Bangkok's American ex-pat community.

Richard was in a corner booth and waved at Frank.

"Well? Easy peasy, right?' he said, grinning at Frank as he sat down. Frank had the cigarette pack in a plastic carrier bag and held onto it tightly. Richard nodded, immediately understanding Frank's expression that told him he wanted to get straight down to business.

"OK, I need to check the goods...in the back." He jerked a thumb behind him towards the toilets.

Frank hesitated for a moment and then slowly pushed the bag across the table and watched as Richard disappeared with it into the restroom. A waitress took Frank's order for a beer and then he waited, trying to ignore the growing tension in his stomach. He needed that money badly and as he closely watched the toilet door, began to wonder what would happen if the man called Greg and just given him a normal carton of cigarettes, with no gems. Frank hadn't checked them. Deep down, he hadn't wanted to know.

The door opened and Richard made his way back towards him, expressionless. Easing back into the booth, he placed the carrier bag onto the bench next to him. His hand moved under his shirt and he unclipped a shoulder money pouch and handed it over to Frank.

"Sorry about the sweat, mate. But it's all good. Here's what we agreed."

Frank took the pouch and checked the contents under the table. He allowed an internal sigh of relief at the sight of the notes inside.

"Have you ever been to a Thai boxing match, Frank?"

****

The atmosphere was heavy with smoke and the cries of a thousand Thai yelps as the opponents literally kicked the shit out of each other. Their combination of punching and kicking blurred fast and furious in the caged ring, jabbing at each other like furious cockerels.

Richard turned to Frank, sweat glistening on his forehead. "This is what it's all about, eh Frank?"

Frank nodded silently, unsure of a reason to argue.

"So, why could Greg or someone else not have brought them up?"

"Simple logistics, Frank," said Richard. "Yes, any number of people could do it, but people I work with are very busy. Also, I need Greg in the south at all times. Anyway, I trust your face and you're from the old country." He patted Frank on the back in a jovial gesture of friendship.

At that moment a short, stocky Thai man came up and spoke to Richard in Thai. Frank couldn't hear them anyway and continued to watch the match. The man in the blue corner was getting the upper hand and getting kicks and punches through his opponent's defence.

"Frank, this is Police Lieutenant General Chatri Anuwat of the Thai Royal police, for the Bangkok province."

Frank shook hands and felt slightly unnerved that Richard was introducing him to a Thai policeman, a very high level one at that.

As if reading his mind, Richard winked at him. "It's OK."

The police lieutenant smiled at Frank but said nothing. His eyes studied him for a moment before returning to the boxing ring. He drank some kind of liquor from a paper cup and was approached by another Thai man who took a wad of Thai Baht notes from him. Frank guessed that the police lieutenant was having a fairly hefty bet on the outcome.

CHAPTER 12

Richard walked past the Grand China Hotel on Thanon Yaowarat and then crossed the busy road that bustled with Chinese street traders hawking their exotic Asian dishes. He stepped into a secluded bar and moved slowly to the back, looking around for someone. His eyes took a while adjusting to the low lit interior which was illuminated with dark blue and pink lights fixed inside paper lanterns. Finally, he saw the familiar, smartly dressed figure of a striking mixed race man with shoulder length hair sitting in an alcove near the back.

"Hello, Theo."

"Hello Richard," said Theo, acknowledging him curtly.

Richard sat down on the expansive leather seat and signalled the waitress for a drink.

"So, how is our friend?" asked Theo.

"He's made contact. He's in. I had him do an easy courier job from the South," Richard replied, evidently pleased with himself.

"Good," said Theo in a matter of fact manner.

"He mentioned a friend called Jimmy Duffy, who might be up for something."

Theo didn't mention he already knew who Jimmy was and had arranged the theft of both their possessions and money in Koh Samui. Unfortunately, Jimmy hadn't been so careless to leave his main valuables in his hut. But with Frank almost out of money he was more likely to take up Richard's offer.

"That is good to know. Does Frank trust you?" Theo took a slug of beer, his sharp blue eyes settling on the Englishman.

"Yeah, I think so."

"Well, he had better. We'll probably need his friend too," Theo whispered.

"So what's this all about?" Richard asked, before immediately holding up his hands in a defensive gesture. "Sorry, I know I shouldn't ask."

Theo ignored him and fished a five hundred baht note out of his wallet, tossing it onto the table next to his half-finished beer and stood up.

"I'll be seeing you," he said and walked off. Richard held his beer up, glancing sideways as Theo disappeared past him. "Great to see you too, Theo," he said.

CHAPTER 13

Frank walked along the Thanon Yaowarat road and glanced up at the address Richard had given him. It was an old, dilapidated, concrete building with a heavy steel door. A metal plaque had the name, 'Stokes Consultancy' etched into it, with an intercom just underneath.

For the past few days, Frank had been weighing up Richard's latest offer. "It's great money," he had said. "Less than a day's work and a trip on an aeroplane," Richard had grinned as if that was the icing on the cake.

"It doesn't involve drug or gem smuggling does it, Rich? Because you can bloody well forget it."

"Absolutely not, Frank! It's completely legal, working with Asian Government agencies. The only reason this has come up at all is because I know people in Government circles."

Frank figured it was worth hearing them out. The alternative, as a sympathetic Swedish traveller listening to Frank's woes had suggested, was selling his passport and reporting it stolen to get a replacement. A Swede called Bernt knew an African gang and he could make the introductions. Frank did not even consider it but he was worried about his finances.

The gem run hadn't paid that much and he knew his cash wouldn't last. There wasn't even enough to get back home. The alternative was to run crying to the British Embassy and he didn't fancy that at all.

Frank pressed the buzzer.

"Good afternoon."

"It's Frank. To see Richard Stokes."

"Hi, Frank."

The door buzzed and Frank let himself in. Richard had explained to him that he used different names. A vital contingency in his line of work, he had explained.

Inside the sparse room, there were two desks and a large table, as well as various computers, phones and a fax machine. Richard greeted Frank with a smile and a handshake and introduced him to the Thai police lieutenant he had met at the boxing match, who once again smiled and said nothing.

"This is Dean Whiteman." Richard gestured to a tall, officious, western man in a grey suit who peered at Frank through his gold-rimmed glasses.

"How do you do, Frank? Thanks for coming," he smiled and gave Frank a firm handshake.

Richard offered everyone drinks, said a few words and then handed over to Whiteman.

"I'm from the Legislative Council of Hong Kong. We are mainly dealing with the transfer of Hong Kong to Chinese rule in 1997. However, we've been asked to help the Hong Kong authorities and the Special Duties Unit test their counter-terrorism responses in a drill."

Whiteman paused and sipped from a glass of water.

"What we're basically looking for are volunteers to help with the exercise. You will be compensated and I'll come onto that in a moment."

Frank glanced around at the group of men. He remembered Carl had once mentioned something about similar drills taking place in England. It made sense.

"The exercise will involve various journeys that must take place at a certain date and time. I can't emphasise the importance of this enough."

Frank nodded in agreement.

"We'll pay you $5000 US and naturally you will receive the travel expenses to Hong Kong. Half in advance. It'll be a same day return flight so no accommodation is needed. Does that sound agreeable so far?" asked Whiteman.

Frank leaned back in his chair. "May I ask why this has all

been arranged in Bangkok and what the Thai police connection is?"

"Fair question, Mr Bowen. Exercises such as these are carried out throughout Asia, usually as a planned blueprint. So each nation, and this has included South Korea, Vietnam and Malaysia, have an agreement to share intelligence when it comes to counter-terrorism. The agreement includes exercises of this kind."

He paused again and, when no one spoke, continued: "Your reference to the Royal Thai police and the police Lieutenant General here, simply ties in with that. That's really all I can say without breaching confidential information."

Frank nodded his head, satisfied. "Ok."

"Richard mentioned you may be able to bring in a friend. We need two people for the exercise ideally. It's the same deal for him if he's interested?"

"I should be able to get hold of him, I'll ask," said Frank.

"Good. It has to happen on the 2nd of February, which is one week from today. As I said, dates, times and places are very, very important. There are a lot of resources being devoted to this. Do you understand?"

"Yes loud and clear. Like I said, I'm happy to do it. I need the money to stay out here for a bit longer and then get back home," said Frank.

"Great. Any further questions?"

Frank shook his head.

"Richard will brief you on the details and will give you all the documents you need."

With that, Dean Whiteman shook hands with Frank and left the room.

Richard smiled at Frank, patted him on the shoulder and offered another round of drinks. The remaining men in the room seemed to eye him with a curious regard.

****

The next morning, Frank managed to track down the number of the hostel where Jimmy was staying. He had already moved on but had left a forwarding phone number as promised.

Eventually, Frank got through and filled Jimmy in with the details.

"Sounds like it'll be worth looking at. I certainly need the money, Frank. It'd be great to catch up again anyway. I'll get the overnight to Bangkok."

Jimmy Duffy met with Frank a few days later, as arranged at his guesthouse, and they caught up over a few beers.

"So it's all kosher then, you think, Frank? I can't afford to get into any murky waters. I didn't mention my ma. She's sick. Breast cancer. I received a letter last week. So after this, I'm off back home."

Frank looked pained and leaned over to put on a hand on Jimmy's shoulder. "Jimmy, I'm really sorry to hear that mate. You should get back there and be with her."

"It's ok. I need the money. I can use it to help her or take her on holiday. Hey, any excuse to stay in the sun, eh?" he said, winking at his friend.

Looking out onto the street he was facing, Frank watched a group of builders as they scurried along rickety bamboo scaffolding as if they were on a tightrope. He had gone over the details with Richard and it all made sense to him. The money would keep him on the travel trail for a long while yet. He could do the rest of Asia and then the rest of the world beckoned. Australia, New Zealand? The prospect was truly exciting.

"If you're absolutely sure, Jimmy?"

The Irishman nodded.

"OK. It's just an exercise; which is pretty common in most countries. I know my friend who works at MI6 said it was pretty standard practice at home," Frank said.

"Well, if you're happy, I'm happy. Here's to Hong Kong, Frank."

The two men clinked beer bottles to their new found adventure.

CHAPTER 14

The plane from Bangkok banked a hard left as it came into Hong Kong International Airport at Kai Tak that jutted out into Kowloon Bay over the impressive skyline. It was touted as one of the world's most dramatic air descents and the two men would certainly have agreed with that as they stared at the sky-high buildings flashing past their window.

As instructed, Frank and Jimmy parted company at the airport terminal, shaking hands and confirming their meet rendezvous, before Frank headed out to find a taxi. The flight had been late and neither of them had time to lose. Frank waited in line for about ten minutes and jumped in with his small backpack when one became available.

"Tsim Sha Tsui star ferry please."

Studying his map carefully, Frank plotted out his route once again. He needed to take the short ferry journey across to the island and from there get the 11.30am MTR train to Causeway Bay. He glanced at his watch which read 10:45. He was already sailing close to the wind.

The taxi crawled along the road and Frank looked across at Kowloon, shimmering in the dusty heat. Eventually, they reached the Kai Tuk tunnel where bright sunshine was replaced by the artificial glare of the tunnel lights. They reappeared onto the East Kowloon corridor and headed towards the west of the city, where ramshackled buildings, covered in Chinese graffiti, towered over them on each side.

After cutting through a number of side streets, they rounded a corner and the majestic scene of Hong Kong Island, with modern, jutting skyscrapers and the mountainous peaks behind them, came into view.

At the ferry terminal, Frank paid the driver and joined the crowds of locals mixed with tourists, moving slowly through the turnstiles into the waiting area.

Climbing up to the upper deck Frank leaned against the rail, gazing across the water as the ferry began its short journey. Another ferry passed them; heading in the opposite direction and a tugboat scooted across their path up ahead.

He glanced at his Omega for the umpteenth time. The layered ferry terminal slated on concrete pillars grew closer and Frank moved towards the exit bay to get off quickly. Once clear of the departing crowd he jogged towards the main Connaught Road, asking general directions on the way, hardly waiting for the details. After getting lost for five precious minutes, Frank spotted the entrance and ran down the steps, joining a small queue at a ticket office. The time was 11.28am; he had two minutes. It was the train he had to get, no earlier, no later. That was the instruction.

He wished he had pushed for an earlier flight as his heart pumped in his chest, waiting behind an old woman, as she spoke to the official behind the glass.

Finally, she had her ticket and Frank stepped up to the booth quickly, ordering his, before bolting through the turnstile. His quickening steps weaved through people on the escalator down to the platform, where he caught a glimpse of the last passengers getting onto his train. The doors clunked shut just as his feet reached the smoothly polished platform.

Frank swore out loud as the train moved steadily away from him. He watched the glint of the end carriage disappear into the darkness, the rumble on the tracks fading until it had disappeared completely, leaving him staring at the dark red tiles of the tunnel wall.

"There goes five grand," he said out loud, dropping his haversack onto the ground in despair. "Shit!"

Frank loitered for a while, pacing the platform and then decided to leave the station. He walked back out onto the road and briefly glanced into a bar with a television that had attracted a small crowd. It was time to think this through and figure out how he was going explain this screw-up and, more importantly, figure how he could get the rest of the money.

The smoke filled bar was darkly lit, despite the hour, and he nodded to the barman who was making himself busy whilst glancing at the nearest television screen.

Frank sipped his beer and tried to think. All he could do was meet Jimmy at the rendezvous hostel and take it from there. His eyes wandered to the screen that a group of Chinese businessmen and locals were watching so avidly.

The anchorman spoke hurriedly in the local dialect against backdrop footage of rising smoke coming from a familiar skyline. Hong Kong's skyline. The shot changed to a reporter on the street talking to the camera. Behind him was a scene of chaos with policemen, ambulance crews and wounded civilians.

What followed next ran an ice cold chill through Frank's entire body—a still photographic mug shot of his friend, Jimmy Duffy, suddenly filled the screen.

CHAPTER 15

An hour earlier, Jimmy Duffy jumped onto the double-decker, North Point bound tram right on schedule. He looked around the crowded space and grabbed a free hand rest dangling down, before peering out at the busy King's Road. The tram faithfully followed the snake-like rail line into the Chun Yeung Street market.

Jimmy checked the next stop on the map and confirmed that it was his. He jumped off the tram as it slowed down and started to walk back, past the endless food stalls that grabbed the interest of passing tourists and locals alike.

"A quick coffee and I'm done," he thought.

The force of the explosion that ripped through the busy street from behind threw him onto the ground. The dense shockwave seemed to run through his entire body. Jimmy lay still for a few seconds, hearing nothing but a high pitched tone deep inside his ears. He slowly turned onto his side and looked back at the tram he had just stepped from and saw it was opened up like a sardine can. The roof spewed dense smoke, billowing into the sky.

For a moment, he supposed that somehow this was all part of the exercise. His brain trying to make sense of what his eyes were seeing.

That notion didn't last very long as, to his utter horror, he saw moving figures inside the burning carriage, flapping around wildly as they tried to escape.

Jesus Christ.

People lay huddled on the ground and then he saw the body parts, burnt clothes strewn across the road and pavement. A dense, sickening smell invaded Jimmy's throat and he turned and vomited hard and fast.

A woman staggered around screaming, part of her arm was missing and thick blood sprayed uncontrollably from the wound.

The smoke spread across the entire area like an attacking fog, turning the busy street –that had been enjoying a sunny afternoon – into hell on earth.

A bomb? Why a real bomb?

And then Jimmy realised.

He used all his strength to get onto his knees and felt wetness on the back of his trousers. Dark red liquid spread fast. He hacked and coughed as the smoke reached him, rushing past and spreading into nearby buildings and shops.

****

Thirty minutes previously, Lieutenant Chan of the SAS trained Hong Kong Special Duties Unit, or the 'Flying Tigers' as they were nicknamed, had listened closely to his earpiece. His four-man team had been on standby for several hours. Fully briefed, each man was in position one level up in the small hotel overlooking the Chun Yeung Street market.

All Chan knew from his superiors was that they had to focus on one man, whatever happened. The tip-off was that a dangerous Caucasian man was likely to be in the area at the time of the explosion and most likely to be on the tram. In the unlikely event of him surviving, they were to take him out.

When the explosion ripped through the street, Chan and his men were initially surprised, despite having forewarning but their professionalism rapidly kicked in and the job in hand became paramount.

"Ok let's go!"

Agent Xeng scanned the square through his field glasses. His colleague, watching through the sighting of his Lee-Enfield L42A1 sniper rifle, also scanned the street around the scene of the explosion. The two agents were positioned in a building that looked down the market street at the rear of the burning tram. The billowing smoke had started to obscure Xeng's vision and he caught glimpses of burning bodies and bloodied limbs, strewn on the concrete road. Several screams filtered back down the street. He breathed deeply and swallowed hard, trying to concentrate and stay focused. In his entire fifteen-year career, he had never seen anything like the scene that lay before him now.

He watched his fellow colleagues, dressed in black combat gear with helmets and night vision visors, holding their Colt Automatic Rifles in attack mode as they moved, one at a time, towards the scene of the explosion. Occasionally pausing behind street stalls, they checked ahead before moving forward again. Frightened civilians who were crouching or had been thrown onto the ground looked at them in astonishment.

"Any sighting, Bravo 9?"

"No, nothing yet. I ...wait!" As he was speaking, Xeng caught sight of what looked to be their target. He was a large man in a white shirt and on the ground on the far side of the tram. Then, drifting smoke obscured his vision.

"Ten metres ... keep going to the corner, he's right there."

Chan moved to the edge of the building and glanced behind him. Sun was right with him and the other two agents were on the opposite side, covering them both. He caught his breath and quickly looked around the corner, seeing the target at once and just as fast, moved his head back again.

Chan gestured silently with his hand, pointing it towards the tram and Sun moved quickly across behind the burning carcass of the carriage to the other side. A young teenage girl on the ground held out an arm towards the running figure, but he ignored her.

"Agent Sun, can you get a shot on the target?" Chan spoke firmly into his radio.

"Too much smoke, Lieutenant"

"Xeng. Can you see the target?"

"Yes, target has not moved; looks like he is wounded."

"Can you see a weapon?"

"Negative. But the smoke is getting worse."

"Ok Agent Sun, let's do it."

Chan moved around the corner, moving slowly toward the

man as Sun simultaneously moved in the same direction from the other side of the burning tram.

****

Out of the mist, Jimmy saw a tall, padded, dark figure, closely followed by another figure a few metres apart. They wore some kind of gas masks, or visors, and were pointing their weapons directly towards him.

The fatigued clad figure closest to him seemed to adjust his weapon. Jimmy held his hands up and opened his mouth to speak; to tell them he'd been duped and this wasn't part of the plan. No words left his mouth.

Jimmy Duffy's last vision was a flickering flash from the muzzle of the assault rifle aimed at his head.

CHAPTER 16

Frank moved into an alcove at the back of the bar where another television was streaming an English version of the news. He strained to listen to the low volume.

"...Tram explosion on Chun Yeung Street market. No reports yet of the number of casualties."

The live footage showed a bird's eye view of the square with smoke billowing up alongside the city's skyscrapers. The tiny red and blue flashing lights of dozens of ambulance and security vehicles peppered the screen.

Frank's shaking hand could barely hold the beer bottle and he placed it on a table. His mind raced. The same mug shot of Jimmy filled the screen once again.

"Reports are coming in from eyewitnesses that police engaged and shot a western Caucasian man at the scene. We are still waiting for a statement from the Special Duties Unit."

Frank's head fell into his hands and he felt utterly crushed. Total confusion, fear and panic all seemed to combine into a potent cocktail of emotion, rushing through him like an injection of some powerful vaccination. He gripped the edge of the table hard and tried to clear his head, fighting the welling tears.

Think Frank, Think!

He and Jimmy had been set-up big-time. How the bomb had been planted on the tram he had no idea, but he was certain Jimmy wasn't carrying any device. It must have been there already, or put into his bag?

An intense fear run through him and his heart started

pumping hard. His eyes moved down to his haversack. There couldn't be anything in there; he had rummaged through it at the airport. He tried to remember if he had left it unattended at any point and concluded he had not.

Nevertheless, Frank slowly and carefully opened the zip and removed the small number of items, one by one—his wash bag, spare clothing, moneybag and passport. He very carefully searched each of the side pockets. There was nothing out of the ordinary. Frank exhaled slowly.

"...a secondary explosion has been reported at the Causeway Bay MTR station. The East Concourse has been badly damaged."

Frank looked up at the screen.

Causeway Bay! The station he hadn't been able to get to for the arranged time.

I can't believe this!

Frank was fixated on the screen and thought about Jimmy getting shot. That meant he must have been specifically targeted and that also meant Frank was probably in danger too. It was time to disappear fast and get out of sight.

Seeing the gentlemen's toilets, he went inside. He had to change his appearance in any way. With soap lather, he greased back his thick black hair in a way he would never usually have it. He already had a pair of shades and would need to get some kind of hat. Unsure of whether it would make any difference he quickly changed his shirt, just in case it might help make him less recognisable.

Had he already been flagged up as some kind of bomber? Frank didn't particularly want to hang around to find out. He pulled out his wash bag to get freshened up, almost as a way of procrastinating before having to face the streets.

The small piece of card with its scribbled phone number fell out into the sink as he rooted around for his face wash. He stared at it blankly for a second, remembering how, in Goa, he had found it and then stuffed it back inside. It had stayed in there ever since.

Maria.

He remembered her saying she had family or some connection

in Hong Kong. He took the piece of ripped card and put it safely in his wallet. That could well be the only option he had.

CHAPTER 17

A second Special Unit team had been dispatched to Causeway Bay and had split into four groups. The teams were not in full combat gear like their colleagues at the market but wore heavy navy vest jackets hanging over their T-shirts. They also had air-filtered masks hanging from their utility belts.

There were five exits for the station and they were all covered by agents. They mingled with the crowds heading in and out of the station and awaited their orders.

Causeway Bay was one of the most crowded areas in Hong Kong, with a shopping centre above the station that proudly hosted all the big brand shops carrying products from Japan, Europe and the United States.

Team Alpha waited around by the East entrance on Great George Street while Team Beta waited at the West entrance, with other teams covering other exits.

Each two-man team had only just got into position. Team Alpha, which consisted of Charlie Wo and Joe Yi, felt a distant roar and vibration underneath their feet. Both men instantly knew it was no train. Charlie Wo looked at the tall frame of his colleague, "That could be it. Did you feel that?"

"Radio it in," Agent Yi replied gruffly. Charlie nodded and pressed the disponder on the radio strapped to his right shoulder.

"Agent Wo here. We are just in position at the East Concourse and felt a tremor."

There was a slight pause before he received a response. "Move down to the station and look for the target and keep low.

Emergency services are on their way," the radio hissed back at him.

Charlie nodded to his colleague and they quickly moved down the steps towards the underground station. A few metres down the subway, they heard distant screams and a wall of dust came rushing up the corridor, choking the two men and the handful of other people in the area.

Charlie and Joe quickly put on their masks before continuing down to the platform.

A stream of terrified civilians came running from the opposite direction, attempting to escape the scene. The two agents scanned their faces looking for the male Caucasian before gesturing to them to make their way to the exit. The chaos seemed to increase rapidly the nearer they got to the platform and the smoke thickened making it impossible to see anything. Everyone was choking and coughing and Joe spotted the first casualty, a middle-aged woman covered in blood, staggering around in a daze.

"Are you OK, Madame? Emergency services will be here any minute. Please make your way out now," he held her arm and manoeuvred her in the right direction.

"This is crazy!" shouted Joe.

"I know, I know. Keep focused. Remember, this man is supposed to be very dangerous." The target in the photograph they both had was Frank Bowen.

The two agents moved slowly towards the platform, occasionally helping a distressed passenger who had been lucky enough to escape with minor injuries. A chorus of wails and the sound of misery greeted them as they stepped down to the platform that was drenched in blood. They were soon stepping over limbs and bodies. A red heat blew from the carcass of the train that had exploded in the station. The carriages still contained passengers who desperately fought to escape the furnace.

Joe Yi caught his breath in his chest as he looked around at the pandemonium unleashed before him. He immediately depressed his radio disponder.

"Team Alpha at location. No sign of suspect. Multiple casualties. Where are the emergency services?"

"Right behind you. They'll be at the scene any moment. Just keep looking."

An hour later, all the teams reported that there was no sign of their suspect. Dead or alive.

CHAPTER 18

Theo Kampala sat at his desk in the Bangkok Hilton hotel room and prepared to make contact with his superior, agent name Oracle, within the MSS – Chinese intelligence – for just the second time in the year. He scribbled down the coded message, encrypted it and then input the letters into the modified Soviet M-125 Fialka cypher machine. His message: Operation Dizang successful but the Redshank bird has flown.

After sending the message, Theo waited as the crackling radio fizzed against the background hum of the air con.

In Beijing, a radio operator waited patiently, standing to attention in front of the large desk that Ho Zhang sat behind in his officious leather chair. He read the message sent by agent Bashe and was not happy at all. If one of the terrorists had escaped, then how was the operation a success? This had to be dealt with as soon as possible.

Zhang dismissed the operator and then walked to the window and looked across the river towards the hazy cityscape of south Beijing, his mind drifting. His office was in the Hang corporate building and looked exactly as if it was another department in the corporate infrastructure, but of course, it wasn't. No other employees of the Hang Company knew what the department on the 34th floor did.

He paced up and down, weighing his options and then returned to his oak desk to write another message on his notepad. Picking up his phone, he called through the internal line to the radio operator and asked him to return to his office.

"Send this to Agent Bashe," he said, handing the operator the slip of paper.

In Bangkok, Theo watched the Fialka cypher machine spit out the encrypted message onto a sheet of paper; his response from the Beijing station. He ripped off the sheet and translated the encryption.

It was an order to find the escaped bird and clean up. Theo stared at the message. Cleaning up meant tracking down Frank Bowen to kill him.

The television screen showed the latest images from the war in Kuwait. The eyes of the entire world were focused there. The operation seemed to be perfect timing. No doubt they planned that way.

CHAPTER 19

Frank dialled the number from a phone booth that was hidden down a side street. A female voice answered.

"Is that Maria?"

"Yes?"

"Hey, Maria. It's Frank. We never quite got to say goodbye in Goa."

There was a pause.

"Frank? How are you?"

"I'm fine, kind of. Listen, I'm in Hong Kong and wondered if I could see you?"

"Sure, come and visit anytime."

"Erm. Sorry for the short notice, but can I come over now?"

Maria laughed, "Ok, no problem. I'll give you the address."

Frank studied his battered map and thought about the best way to get there. He wasn't sure whether his photo was now plastered all over the media and needed to get to Maria's place undetected. Hopefully, his slightly changed appearance would help. He noticed – with worry – that Happy Valley was fairly close to the Causeway Bay, an area he obviously wanted to avoid.

Frank hailed a taxi and asked for Deep Water Bay on the far side of Hong Kong Island.

Thankfully, after some initial small talk, the driver didn't pay close attention to his passenger, enabling him to lie low in the back seat. The journey seemed to take an age and Frank relaxed once they had reached the island.

At Deep Water Bay, Frank hailed a different cab to the Hong

Kong Cricket Club. He asked the driver to stop nearby and waited until it had disappeared before crossing the main road and climbing secluded steps that weaved up the hill through a wood. The roads were set on hills that offered occasional fantastic panoramic views of the sea and other small islands that appeared merely as grey shapes in the haze. All the low-set houses were protected by walls and gates.

The bell rang, a distant low chiming that seemed to fit perfectly with the calmness and tranquillity of the neighbourhood. It seemed a long way from the hustle and bustle of central Hong Kong. A familiar face answered the door.

"Maria?"

She beamed a welcoming smile that brought back why he had been so attracted to her.

"Hey, Frank. Wow, really nice to see you again."

They hugged and Maria gestured for him to follow her. "Come in."

The house had the typical décor of an expat residence. The wall of the hallway was covered with paintings and photographs of landscape scenes from Amsterdam and London.

Frank heard the distant faint background sound of Budgerigars punctuating through the house. The slow fans whirred overhead as they entered a large living room area with tall windows that overlooked Kowloon. Chinese art, depicting ancient warriors and dragons, hung on the wall and a large, beautifully decorated vase sat on a low table near the door.

"Are you ok?" She looked at him, frowning, sensing the tension in him.

"It's been an insane day, Maria. I'm still taking it all in, to be honest. I need to clear my head and figure out what the hell is going on."

Frank accepted tea and explained the day's events. It sounded unbelievable, even as he uttered the words, but he continued. Maria stared at him in disbelief, her mind obviously whirring like a motor. After he had finished his story her head was in her hands.

Frank looked at her with a hint of harshness. "You *do* believe me, right?"

"Yes Frank, yes, of course." She went over and put her arms around him. She whispered, "What are you going to do?"

"I've got to go through the whole thing. It seems I've been set up as some kind of dupe for this bloody mess and I was obviously supposed to die in that tube explosion. I can't believe I was so stupid. Now I'm some kind of target. Yes, I could give myself up, but everything points to me ... and Jimmy. I can't stop thinking about him. I pulled him into this and now he's dead."

Frank felt the anger rising inside him; anger mixed with desperation and confusion.

"I'm caught bang in the middle of some bullshit. If I give up I'll be framed, I know I will. That bastard Richard set me up. I need to get to Bangkok and find him as soon as possible."

Frank was letting his anger run forth and Maria seemed to know better than to start to argue.

"Who else was in Bangkok?" she asked.

"This Dean Whiteman guy. Very officious. He said he was part of the Legislative Council of Hong Kong."

"Wait a minute, yes. My father works for them. Remember me telling you? Maybe he can help."

"I doubt very much that this Mr Whiteman was part of that department; he was just a very slick conman but it might be worth checking out. There was also a Thai police lieutenant. I can't remember his bloody name."

Maria frowned. "That's pretty high up in the police rank. Was he in on it, do you think?"

Frank shook his head.

"No idea." He looked up at Maria. "Listen, do you think your father could get me a passport? A fake one, I mean?"

Maria paused, "Hmm, I'm not sure. I'll try, Frank. He's actually coming by soon, so you can meet him."

"Great. I stashed most of the money they paid me in Bangkok, thinking I'd go back there. Maybe I should get it back. I think I'm gonna need it."

Maria stroked his arm. "Hmm, that all sounds a bit dangerous at the moment. Please don't worry about money, I can lend you some."

"Thanks, Maria, that's appreciated. But I also need to track down this Richard guy."

"I don't think that's a great idea either."

Frank stood up and walked to the window, staring across the city skyline.

"I know it's not a great idea but … shit, I don't know what to do," he said.

"The British Embassy?"

"No. It's too risky. I don't know who's involved." He turned to Maria. "You know what's so funny about this mess? I was running for that train like my life depended on it and if I had caught it I'd most likely be dead now. That's pretty ironic, huh?"

CHAPTER 20

Christopher Johnson, Chief Inspector of the Royal Hong Kong police force, shifted through the report shared with his department by the Counter Terrorism Response Unit telling him there was a second Caucasian terrorist at large in his city.

He stared at a photograph of Frank Bowen. According to the report, his suspected connections included MI6, the Ulster Defence Association in Northern Ireland and various drug cartels, although no direct evidence was offered for this. He was also deemed very dangerous. It claimed that he had been involved in various criminal activities from an early age and in 1988 – facing drug trafficking charges – had co-operated with the authorities to help bring a larger network of criminals to justice.

However, Johnson could see no reference to actual criminal records or the specific trial mentioned. He frowned and quickly clicked and rotated a pen in his hand over and over.

His team was scanning C.C.T.V. footage at that very moment but nothing had come up so far. The Police were also watching all main transport hubs and he had ordered extra men to patrol the city.

Johnson picked up the phone and asked for Lim Su Sung, his senior inspector of police, to come into his office. After five minutes, Lim knocked on the open door and entered. He was a tall, prominent figure, wearing round glasses, and a workaholic who had served well for the force. The two men had worked together for over five years.

"Hi Lim, have you looked through this?" said the chief inspector, gesturing to the report in front of him.

"Yes, I read through it."

"It came through from the local MI6 station," the chief said, almost as a question.

"Apparently so, Sir."

"Take a seat." He gestured to the chair opposite him and the senior inspector dutifully sat down and looked at the chief expectantly.

"It's interesting that MI6 passed on this information so readily. It's not their usual style."

"Yes and very quickly too," agreed Lim.

"I know it's not usual practice, Lim, but can you get in touch with your point of contact in London and get confirmation of this report for me? Also, request any further information they have on this Frank Bowen."

"Right away, Sir."

****

Detective Inspector Douglas Brown walked down the East Concourse at Causeway Bay station, surveying the echoes of destruction which became starker as he neared the platform. Broken glass, plastic and metal had spread across the polished tiles on the ground, spreading a sea of blackened dust and debris, only punctured by dozens of cut-out shapes where bodies had fallen since removed from the scene. Dried blood had stained wide areas of the platform and the thick atmosphere made Brown feel a wave of claustrophobia for a moment.

He laid his eyes on the charred husk of the train that had every single window blasted out, giving it a ghost-like aura. Where the windows had been; only inky black gaps remained. Yellow ticker tape sealed off entire areas and a white-suited forensic team, with masks and gloves, painstakingly picked through the debris and bagged anything of interest.

Brown carefully stepped over to the train and spoke to the officer in charge who walked him along to the carriage where the explosion had detonated. This carriage, almost in the middle, was blacker than the rest.

"This is where the explosion and the resulting fire were at

their most intense," said the Officer, dryly. "A large fireball ripped through the remaining carriages, both ways."

Brown peered inside, through the blackened gaps of the windows. The plastic passenger seats had melted into unrecognisable shapes and the whole floor seemed to have been ripped upwards as if some incredible force had punched its way through. Shards of metal from the train floor streaked in all directions. Brown couldn't begin to imagine what it had been like to be caught up in this horror.

The detective inspector took an hour looking around the scene, taking notes and mopping his brow with a handkerchief to wipe away the floating dust that clung to his skin, before walking back up the concourse. He found his car and sat in it for a moment, breathing heavily, trying desperately to dispel the nausea.

He glanced at himself in the car mirror; his swept back, grey hair seemed to him to be verging on white and he adjusted his thick-rimmed, black spectacles. He had definitely aged rapidly since moving to Hong Kong, he noticed solemnly.

Swapping from the London Met to the Royal Hong Kong force was not something he had expected five years before, but meeting his Chinese wife on a holiday break in Hong Kong had set him on an entirely different path in life. She worked in a department store, a fashionista. Yet her feet were firmly on the ground and he loved her for it. Funny how life turned out if you were open to change, he'd thought, and the moment that he decided 'to hell with it' would always stick in his mind. He married the girl and put in for a transfer.

Hong Kong was not without its problems. Triad activity seemed to be on the increase and a new kind of anxiety had gripped the city, especially with the Chinese handover six years away. And now it looked like a new fear was going to close in; the fear of terrorism.

The detective inspector started the engine and headed west, skirting around Victoria Park, then along King's Road towards Chun Yeung Street market and another scene of carnage.

CHAPTER 21

Maria's father walked into her living room. He was tall and cut an imposing, confident figure. His cropped silver hair was a stark contrast to his tanned skin and he wore a dark suit with a white shirt, no tie. The man stared at Frank for a moment with a hint of surprise which quickly turned to a broad smile.

"This is my friend, Frank," said Maria, before turning to Frank. "And this is my dad, Peter."

"Pleased to meet you, Frank." Both men shook hands. Peter Chapman spoke with the confidence of a man who knew what he wanted and how to get it.

Frank felt an uneasy tension for a moment as if Peter was aware of what he was about to ask. Perhaps Maria had mentioned something to him on the phone?

Maria made some green tea and they sat around the coffee table in the breakfast room that held a spectacular view across Tai Tam Country Park. The clock chime signalled the passing of another hour from the hallway.

"First time in Hong Kong?" asked Peter, carefully pouring tea into each cup as if it were a practiced art.

"It is." Frank felt unable to elaborate further and instead asked permission to smoke. Peter waved him on, his face impassive and unreadable. He finished the tea and his blue eyes moved onto the stranger in his daughter's house.

"So, I'm in a situation," Frank began. "Some kind of messed up intelligence exercise I got involved in. I take it you've seen the news?"

Peter nodded, "I have." He clasped his hands together in front of himself, elaborating no further and instead crooked his head slightly, signalling Frank to continue.

After going through the story once again, Frank drained his tea and fixed Peter with a level stare. "I have been completely stitched up and now I'm in serious trouble but I was definitely nothing to do with what happened. You do understand, Mr Chapman?"

Peter simply nodded in acknowledgement and then turned his teacup on the saucer and took a sip. Placing it back on the glass table top, he leaned back in his chair.

"Well. It certainly sounds serious. I'm tempted to say you need to get to the British Embassy, but I'm sure you've already thought of that."

"Yes," Frank replied, "But right now I don't know what I'm dealing with or who's involved. I just want to get a passport in another name so I can get out of here. I need to figure things out."

"To be perfectly honest it sounds like you could have been a bit more wary before making the decision to do this...exercise."

"It all looked legitimate. They had the credentials, the paperwork. There was no reason to think I would be set up and put on some death list," said Frank, raising his voice slightly. He knew he had been foolish and suddenly felt the need to justify his decision.

Maria's father leaned forward and stared at Frank sternly.

"I don't want my daughter mixed up in this, you hear me?"

Frank held up his hands. "Believe me; I didn't know what else to do. I don't want that either. I just want to figure this out."

"Dad! He needs help. He's not just some guy I met whilst..." Maria seemed to catch herself and quickly looked away.

Her father gave her a sideways glance, leaned back in his chair again and settled his eyes back onto Frank. He exhaled slowly as if making a considered decision.

"I cannot afford to get directly involved in this either, as I'm sure you'll understand. But, as you are a friend of my daughter, I want to help, of course. I can give you a name of someone who can help you. But that's all."

"I understand and am really grateful for your help Peter," said Frank. He glanced at Maria who smiled at him reassuringly.

"Also, I know this is a long shot," Frank continued, "as he probably used a fake name, but there was a man calling himself Dean Whiteman in Bangkok. He appeared to be in charge of the exercise and said he worked for the same Council as you." Frank described the man he had met as Peter and Maria listened.

"Hmm, can't say I know anyone with that name or description, but I'll ask around for you if you like."

Frank nodded, relieved at the feeling that he had some support, no matter how small.

****

The following afternoon, Frank walked through hanging beads into the cramped store that seemed to be stacked high with everything from toasters to Chinese lanterns. It was empty of people and Frank moved to the counter glancing around at the ceiling high stacked consumer goods. Jasmine incense lingered in the air.

A distant sound of a babbling television drifted through a door behind the counter and then, unexpectedly, a face of an older woman appeared, eyeing Frank suspiciously.

Frank put down a black card onto the counter and she glanced at it without picking it up. She turned and shouted in Chinese into the back room. A young man appeared with a cigarette hanging from his mouth, dressed in a vest that had seen cleaner days and yellow knee length shorts. The older woman disappeared behind the back again.

"Hi there. I'm Frank." He gestured to the card on the counter. The young Chinese picked up the card and peered at it for a second.

"Friend of Peter?" he asked, narrowing his eyes at Frank, yet clearly unhappy that this foreigner was standing in his store.

"That's right. He's helping me and I wondered if you could too?" asked Frank, hoping that the visit wasn't going to turn into a waste of time. He had to get this passport.

The young man certainly knew Peter Chapman. His father, a successful Hong Kong businessman, held him in high esteem. The English expat had helped him secure a contract with a

British company and, in the spirit of the Chinese term "guanxi" – a favour for a favour – this was obviously repayment time.

Eventually, the young man nodded and lifted up the counter hatch to let Frank through. They walked through more cluttered rooms and Frank saw the old woman sitting on a sofa watching the television. She glared at Frank and said something in Chinese. The young man shouted back and soon they were walking down some steps into a basement which housed, even more, boxes of televisions and other white goods.

At the back of the windowless basement room, was a clear space with a desk, a filing cabinet and piles of papers. The young man gestured for Frank to sit in an old armchair while he slumped down behind the desk.

"I'm Li," he said, briskly.

"I'm Frank," Frank said for the second time. "I need a passport."

Li nodded. "It will cost five thousand US dollars and I need you to supply a photograph."

Frank shifted uncomfortably in his chair.

"Five thousand? Your friend ... our friend, Peter, said you would help me out. I wasn't expecting it to cost that much," Frank stared at Li apprehensively.

"It's a risky business. Cannot be done cheaply. But you friend of Peter, so let's say two thousand."

That's quite a drop from five thousand, thought Frank. He decided not to look a gift horse in the mouth and pulled out a wad of notes that was rolled into tubes. Maria had kindly lent him the money.

"Ok, I'll give you a grand now and the rest on delivery," said Frank, handing over a roll.

Li considered the money and then grabbed it. "Sure, no problem with that. You have photograph?"

Frank handed over a passport photo he had taken earlier that day in his new look of combed-back hair with the beginnings of a beard he was growing.

"And the name?" asked Li.

Frank thought for a moment. "Make it Joseph Burns, that's all I can think of."

Li nodded and wrote down the name. "No problem. A few days, OK?"

"Thanks for helping me out, Li."

CHAPTER 22

"Hello Carl," said the voice at the other end of the line. Carl recognised Frank's tone immediately and sensed a hint of tension.

"Frank? How are you? Back already?"

"Not quite. I need your help with something."

"Sure, no problem."

"I need you to find out some information for me, on some names. I can't explain everything right now, but I'm in a spot of bother. Life or death situation, mate."

"Oh right? I'm sorry to hear that. I'll try to help you as much as I can, Frank. Is there anything you can tell me?"

Frank paused on the line, the cogs in his brain turning.

"The fact is, I'm finding it hard to trust anyone, possibly even you, so I can't really say too much. It's connected to that Hong Kong thing. I was set up."

"Frank, what the hell's going on? Did you say Hong Kong? I read something about a couple of bombs but it wasn't widely reported here. There's a war in the Gulf that has everyone's attention."

"Yeah. Look, can you help me or not? If I give you some names, can you look into them?"

Carl paused and flicked his pen around in his fingers.

"Of course I'll do what I can, Frank. I don't want to get into trouble though."

"No, it's just getting background information on some names. They set me up, said it was a drill. Richard Desmond – also called himself Richard Stokes – based in Bangkok. There was another man, Dean Whiteman who said he worked for the Legislative Council of Hong Kong. If there's anything you can find out about them, that would be appreciated, Carl. I don't know if these are real names though. I'll ring back sometime tomorrow if I can."

"Sure, but Frank, that's not a lot to go on…"

The line went dead.

Carl replaced the handset and thought for a moment, frowning heavily.

CHAPTER 23

Chiu Wah On – or agent Tian, as was his codename – stamped on the cigarette butt and ground it into the concrete with his heel. The message had come through at his safe house to go deliver on his orders—the moment he had been patiently waiting for. He strolled briskly across the road and pushed back the beads that hung in the doorway.

The young Li looked up from his newspaper at the smart gentleman entering the store. He presumed he was a white-collar worker. His second thought was this man was no ordinary office worker, judging by the long scar that arced prominently on his face.

Chiu smiled warmly at the young man as he cast his eyes around at the stacked wares for sale. A sudden movement caught Li unaware and the man grabbed the back of his head and smacked it down onto the counter in one swift action. He felt the cool butt of a gun pressed against his temple. Chiu pressed hard against the back of his head, keeping Li in place.

"Listen very carefully. You raise any alarm, shout or struggle, you are a dead man. You do exactly as I tell you and you will live … understand?" Chiu whispered menacingly into his ear.

"Yes understood," Li mumbled. His face was pushed so hard against the wood he could hardly speak. Chiu pulled his head back up.

"Now shut the shop."

Li did as he was ordered and flipped the sign over to display 'closed.' His mind raced; so many questions. But for now, he decided just to co-operate.

They moved behind the counter, out of sight from the street and into the back room, the man signalling for Li to sit at the table.

"Your Western friend, where is he?"

Li hesitated, scared, but he knew straight away who this man was referring to—his recent visitor from Peter Chapman, his father's friend.

"Western friend? I know quite a few expats."

Chiu took out a photograph from his inside jacket pocket and held it up in front of Li's face.

"No, I don't recognise him."

"Do not lie to me, my friend, otherwise I promise you will not see out the next minute." The scar-faced man levelled his gun towards Li's face. His eyes seemed to darken, like dead coals.

Li glanced at the gun; his heartbeat seemed to speed up in his chest. He believed what this man was saying, yet his instinct was telling him to keep as much information from him as possible, especially the connection with Peter Chapman. On the other hand, he didn't want to die.

Li closed his eyes. "He came here, into the shop. That is correct."

He felt the gun barrel slowly press against his forehead. Li dared not open his eyes, as though looking at death would somehow encourage it.

"He came in for a fake passport," Li spoke slowly, wishing he wasn't speaking the words that came from his mouth. "He picked it up this morning."

"Show me," the calm voice replied.

****

Theo Kampala picked up his latest message, translated the encryption and then burned the piece of paper. He quickly packed a small bag, placed the encryption machine in a case and left his small room, glad to be on the move, and stepped onto the busy Bangkok street. He hailed a taxi and headed to the train station, watching the blur of traffic swirl around him.

The train station was the usual scene of chaos and he shuffled his way up the line to buy his ticket south. Theo figured Frank

Bowen, hunted like a dog, might end up at a familiar hideaway. The same place Richard Desmond had sent him on his gem run.

CHAPTER 24

Detective Inspector Douglas Brown flashed his badge at the policeman who stood guard outside the front of the shop and made his way through to the counter and then down the steps to the basement. A forensic team of two, dressed in white overalls and masks, were just finishing up their procedure of sweeping for prints and blood samples. Li's body was at the centre of the room, sat upright and slumped against a pile of boxes, his head hanging forward. He had been shot in the head from the front. A claret red splash cast a stark pattern against the cardboard box behind him. His hands were bound behind his back with cord and his feet were also tied.

Brown nodded grimly at the police sergeant at the scene and cast his eyes over the body. 'What have we got?'

"Victim is named Li Wu. Multiple cigarette burns, especially around his face. Fingernails extracted. Looks like he's been tortured for information. Cause of death is most likely the bullet to the head."

"You don't say?"

The sergeant ignored his quip and stood staring straight ahead.

"Not a robbery then?"

"It doesn't look like it at this stage, Sir. Nothing was taken as far as we can see. An eyewitness says he saw a Chinese businessman enter the shop sometime around noon. Another local woman said she came around 12.30 and the closed sign was up."

Brown thought for a moment. "Take down their statements

and then send them to me together with the forensic report when it's ready. What about the victim's family?"

"His mother's in the kitchen with an officer. She was out at the time and came back to find him like this. We are in the process of locating the rest of the family."

"I'll talk to her before I leave. Anything else?"

"Yes, crucially there's evidence the victim was involved in passport forgery. A few stamp blocks, lactate film, a variety of blank passports and all the tools. I've gathered them up for evidence."

Brown scanned the gloomy basement one more time. "Thanks, Sergeant." He climbed the steps to the rooms above and spoke briefly with the sobbing mother who had found her son's body, trying to give her some comfort. As he left, Brown asked the officer with her to ensure a statement was sent to him as soon as possible and then returned to his car.

CHAPTER 25

Distant lights flickered from across the water in Kowloon and, apart from the familiar chorus of crickets and occasional noises escaping from the harbour miles away, the neighbourhood stood in near silence. Chiu crouched low and still, his eyes and ears straining with alertness from behind the large palm leaves, where he waited at the bottom of the garden. His main focus was on the tall windows of the living room. He caught a brief glimpse of a shadow move momentarily across the ceiling before disappearing again.

Maria set down a glass of red wine in front of Frank and slumped down next to him on the living room sofa.

"Thanks," said Frank, sipping the wine slowly. "So do you own this place?"

"My Dad does. I just live here and keep it warm." She patted the sofa arm.

"That's great," Frank almost whispered as he lost himself in the distant city lights.

"I know, I know. I'm such a lucky girl."

"There's nothing wrong with luck," he said. He could sure do with some himself, he thought.

"What's with the horse?" Frank gestured towards a finely sculptured piece, expertly crafted from dark wood that stood defiantly as if standing its ground.

"In Chinese culture, horses symbolise success, courage and loyalty among other things. That particular horse is older than Christ."

"Wow. It must be valuable."

"It is," she smiled, knowingly.

"My kingdom for a horse," he said, drily. Maria wrinkled her nose and laughed. Frank smiled at her and studied her face. The perfect lines of her eyebrows shaped to perfection, and the delicate tilt of her lips seemed to comfort him, as if everything was normal and fine, just for that moment. Her green eyes seemed to shine and intensify at his gaze, before glancing away, self-consciously.

"I'm sorry about all this, Maria. Barging in on you and everything. I really wished – hoped – the circumstances would be so different."

She took his hand in hers. "Hey, don't worry. It's lovely to see you, Frank. Despite the … crazy circumstances."

Frank pulled her towards him, kissing her gently on the lips. They became lost in each other and for a second Frank had forgotten all his troubles.

He leaned back and gave a satisfied sigh.

"How about some snacks before bed, hmm?" she asked.

"That sounds good."

Maria walked across the room towards the kitchen and then stopped and froze as she glanced towards the hallway door.

Frank looked up at her, "What is it?" He turned towards the direction of her surprised stare to see a Chinese man in a navy boiler suit, half obscured by darkness, pointing a pistol at her. Frank made to get up and the intruder swung round, aiming the weapon at him, which made him stop dead. The man smiled benignly.

"Frank Bowen?" he asked.

"Who the hell are you?" Maria asked. Carefully, the man moved further into the room revealing a cold, hard face; his smooth skin severed by a moon-shaped scar. Maria held her hands up, her face fixed in an expression of fear as she ever so slowly inched forward toward him. "Please don't hurt us, please..." she continued.

The intruder levelled his gun at her, "Stay still."

"What do you want?" Frank asked. He was slowly standing up from the sofa. The Chinese man turned the gun on him, taking his attention away from Maria. "Stay where you are," he rasped.

Whatever he had come for, he seemed to be hesitating.

Maria acted instinctively, without thought of consequence, grabbing the vase resting on the table that she had slowly edged towards. In one swift action, scooping up the ceramic piece, she threw it at the man's head with all her strength. His left shoulder jerked upwards but he failed to protect himself as its full force smashed into the side of his skull. The intruder slumped back towards the wall, off balance, and Frank, seeing he was raising his gun, leapt at him to grab his arm before jerking it upwards, smashing his hand against the wall.

The gun fell onto the sofa and Frank followed up with a quick punch to the intruder's stomach as hard as he could, bringing his full body weight in behind the blow. The man's stomach was hard, well protected by muscle, but the force of Frank's punch still made him keel over and groan out loud.

Despite his obvious nausea and disorientation, the Chinese hurled himself at Frank, keeping his head low as he butted his chest. The momentum threw Frank backwards onto the coffee table, crashing the wine bottle and glasses onto the floor. Suddenly there was a hand on Frank's throat, gripping tighter around his larynx so he could not breathe properly. Before he lost control of the situation, Frank fiercely jerked his knee into the intruder's groin. The grip loosened and now it was his turn to gasp for air.

Maria quickly moved over to the sofa and grabbed the weapon. She went around behind the Chinese, whacking him hard across the back of the skull with the pistol butt, grunting with the effort. His head slumped onto Frank's chest like a rag doll as the fight in him suddenly receded and then she quickly changed the gun around in her hands and pointed it straight at the back of the intruder's head. Frank slowly hauled the body off the top of him and climbed to his feet. Maria's whole arms were shaking.

"Great work, Maria. It's ok, it's ok," he said, almost whispering.

Maria nodded and handed Frank the pistol.

"Keep an eye on him; we'd better tie him up. I'll go get some rope," she said, finding her composure again.

As Maria left the room, Frank held the weapon in his hand, staring at it. He looked at the Chinese man slumped on the floor and wondered at Maria's calm, but powerful, response to the situation, glad of it, nevertheless.

"Don't you think we should question him?" asked Frank when she returned.

"No. I think we should get out of here," she said.

"Yes, you go to your father. Just..."

"No Frank. I'm coming with you."

Frank shook his head as he wrapped rope around the unconscious intruder. They needed to get out of the house first and then he would argue with her.

CHAPTER 26

Frank and Maria slowly shuffled forward in separate queues towards the customs checkpoint at Kuala Lumpur airport. Frank had his hair greased back and with his maturing dark stubble, his appearance had changed. He clutched the passport he had managed to get from the young man, Li Wu, in Hong Kong. A smart young Malay customs officer, sitting in a box, gestured him forward and checked his passport. He glanced at Frank and back again at the photograph, then swiftly stamped the page and handed it back, nodding without a word.

Frank waited briefly for Maria to come through and they headed to the luggage collection point together, giving each other a reassuring look. Maria had packed hastily after they had tied up the intruder, cleaned the gun of fingerprints and dumped it in the trash in downtown Hong Kong. At the airport, Maria anonymously phoned the police about the Chinese man tied up in her house.

It's not that they were running away, just buying time, as Frank had put it. He had questions he wanted answering, first in Krabi to see if Mr Ron or that Greg character were around and then to Bangkok to see if he could get the money he had stashed. It was a pretty loose, spontaneous and probably insane plan, but neither of them could think of a better option.

Maria insisted on tagging along and had vehemently dismissed going to her father for help, out of hand. Frank hadn't lied to her father when he said he didn't want her involved but Maria wouldn't say goodbye.

They made their way to the exit area of the impressively

modern airport and caught a connecting bus to the railway station, a colonial-era landmark in the heart of Kuala Lumpur. The ticket office under the high canopy roofs sold them their tickets for the overnight sleeper to Hat Yai in Thailand, then they grabbed some refreshments and sat in an air-conditioned waiting hall, sipping their ice teas.

"I just have to go to the bathroom," said Maria, picking up her cotton shoulder bag.

"Sure," Frank nodded.

Frank returned to the thoughts that had been churning around in his mind on the flight from Hong Kong as he watched Maria walk away. He had been wondering about her lightning-fast reaction to the intruder and the ease with which they had overcome this, apparently, well-trained assassin. Maybe she had surreptitiously left him her Hong Kong number as if it were a backup plan to reel him in, if something went wrong, as it had.

Frank glanced around the waiting hall and then strained to see Maria disappearing through the crowd. At the same time, he couldn't really believe that she was involved. She had been nothing but a saviour and had, after all, attacked the intruder. But how had he found them? He knew the location of Maria's house. It didn't make sense.

Frank leaned towards a businessman reading a paper nearby.

"Excuse me, could you just keep an eye on this for one minute?" Frank asked, pointing to Maria's suitcase. The man nodded. Frank took his money bag and left the waiting hall, looking around for Maria.

A train had just come in and streams of people hustled their way towards the exits. Frank moved forward through the crowd and glanced around the platform area. Across towards the exit, he spotted a reflection of Maria in the glass of a café, making a call from one of the phone booths.

CHAPTER 27

Chiu Wah On felt an intense throbbing pain in his head, his whole body felt constrained as if wrapped in a coil and, before even opening his eyes, he knew he was tied up, wrapped in rope. The room was dark, except for the distant lights of the city that cast long shadows across the floor. Chiu tried to move his hands and loosen the rope slightly but it was tightly done. Fragments of broken glass lay scattered around him and he manoeuvred his body so he was sitting upright against the wall.

He breathed in and out, allowing his chest to expand and shrink and then shuffled and shook, slowly loosening the grip of the coiled rope around his torso. With a sliver of more flexibility, he was able to move his body around and get a broken fragment of glass into his hand. Slowly and deliberately, Chiu worked his fingers, sawing at the rope that bound him.

An hour later, the intruder was flexing his arm, repetitively opening and closing his fingers to get rid of the numbness. He looked at his watch; two hours had passed. He searched the room for his gun and, on not finding it, proceeded to search the house for anything else that might give a clue as to where they were headed. Finding nothing, he left the way he had come in and retrieved a small backpack that he'd previously hidden at the bottom of the garden. It was several hundred metres to his car where he retrieved the keys from his pack before driving to the nearest public phone booth.

Chiu spoke in rapid Mandarin to the voice at the other end and recited the passport details that he had forced out of the young Chinese at the shop. Then he hung up and headed to the airport. There was other work to do.

Six hours later, Chiu had checked into a hotel under an assumed identity in Bangkok.

****

After three days of hiding himself in the hotel, Chiu switched off the television and wiped down all the surfaces that he may have touched during his stay there. It was highly unlikely it would be a problem, but he liked to take precautions. He attached a residential services badge to his white shirt and picked up his red canvas bag that had been in the bottom of the wardrobe.

Checking out of the gated hotel under his false identity, Chiu walked up the relatively quiet Sol Prida promenade towards the main Thanon Sukhumvit road. The street gradually became busier as he walked in the fading sun. Street food carts sold their spicy dishes; restaurants and bars competed for business. A couple of office girls glanced at him as they passed. The air hung thick and humid, as it always did.

There was a bar, sheltered by umbrellas that seemed to sink into the sidewalk, with a sign offering happy hour drinks. Chiu slipped onto a table hidden from the road, ordered an espresso in fluent Thai and fixed his eyes on the apartment block opposite.

An hour later, Richard Desmond wiped his brow with a handkerchief as he descended the stairs to his apartment. He was looking forward to getting the payoff for delivering Frank Bowen to Theo's little operation. It would give him some much-needed breathing space as a few debts were starting to get out of hand.

What would happen to Frank? Desmond didn't much care. He was just another sucker tourist who had arrived in the land of Siam looking for adventure, although he was sure his fellow Englishman had a hidden intelligence behind that mask of nonchalance.

Richard's train of thought was interrupted by a knock at the door, which in itself was strange, as no one could get into the building without buzzing first. *Must be that fat prick from next door wanting to borrow something again,* he thought. Desmond peeped through his spy hole and saw the side of a Chinese man, glancing down the corridor.

"Who are you?" he said through the door.

The face – that bubbled into an oval through the fish-eye lens – turned towards the door and smiled.

"Mr Thang ... building maintenance services. I need to look at your air conditioning unit, Sir." He held his identity card to the spy hole.

"Really? You need to look right now?"

"If that is possible, Sir? There is a problem in other apartments and we want to make sure there isn't a possibility of failure during the night."

That would be a nightmare, thought Richard. Air con was the only way to sleep in Bangkok. He unchained the door and opened it. The man smiled at him and picked up a red canvas bag that he had placed on the floor. Richard stood aside and waved him in. He wondered, for a moment, how a service engineer came to get such an ugly scar but thought it might be rude to mention it.

Richard pointed towards the kitchen, "It's in there, pal."

The engineer moved towards the kitchen and glanced around the apartment.

"I hope it won't take long. I just need to check something," he said.

"No problem," Richard said as he turned to walk back into the living room, looking around for his T.V. remote. He found it under a newspaper on the sofa and pointed it at the screen, frowning in surprise as he caught the reflection of the engineer moving silently up behind him.

CHAPTER 28

Detective Inspector Brown shuffled into his desk chair and was glad to see the forensic report from the shop murder waiting on his desk. It told him what had been obvious; that the gunshot had killed the man and he had been dead for three hours by the time the body had been discovered. Various fingerprints had been found – most of which were Li's – but there was another set which had, so far, turned up no matches.

The Detective's phone rang and he picked it up immediately. "Douglas, it's Chris... Can we talk in my office?"

"Sure, Chief Inspector. I'll be right there."

Inspector Brown entered the chief inspector's office and closed the door behind him. The glassed box offered little privacy from the rest of the department, which Chris Johnson hated. He did have blinds, though, and pulled the cord to close them as was his routine.

He smiled at the inspector and gestured for him to sit down.

"Did much come up on that murder in Mercury Street?"

Detective Brown still had the forensic report in his hand and placed it on Johnson's desk. "Light torture followed by a single headshot that killed him. Still running fingerprint searches but nothing has materialised as yet."

The chief nodded and seemed to pause for thought. "I've asked for a meeting with the Special Unit chief in regards to the recent terrorist attacks," he said. Just then, there was a knock at the door; the figure of the staff sergeant was visible through the frosted glass, waiting outside.

"Yes, come," said the chief.

The staff sergeant held a report in his hand, eyes darting between the chief and the inspector. "I thought I'd better get this to Detective Brown as soon as possible."

Johnson gestured to the Detective, "Be my guest."

Brown took the report, dismissed the sergeant and read for a moment. He handed it to the chief who scanned his eyes over it and raised his eyebrows. "As I thought, there is a connection to the attack." The report in his hands featured a grainy photograph of Chiu Won On.

The chief stood up and started pacing the room. "So this Chinese intelligence agent has been placed at the murder of Li Wu, with fingerprints. He was obviously not very careful unless he wanted us to know. This is a very difficult situation, politically."

"Sure, but if he's murdering people in our city he needs to be found. What's your theory?"

"The Intel on those two British men paints them as double agents with criminal elements, but there are no records of any trials or convictions in the UK relating to the charges mentioned. We checked with London on Bowen and Duffy; according to them, they are not on any watch list nor have any records. They're clean." The chief fished around for the MI6 report in his filing cabinet and handed it to Brown.

"Can you look into it, Detective? I'd be interested in your angle."

Brown took the report and started flipping through it before looking up at the chief.

"You think this is fake?"

"It certainly seems that way. If it is, I need to know, especially if Chinese intelligence is involved. Officially, this is counter intelligence territory, but I'm also meeting Teng from the Special Unit to try to get some co-operation. They were at the scene of the attacks soon after and seemed to be privy to this Intel. I want to know what the hell is going on. Can you tag along to this meeting, Douglas?"

Detective Brown looked up from the papers in his hand, "Yes, of course, Sir."

CHAPTER 29

Raksami – or 'Mr Ron', as he was better known – stepped into his small house just outside of Krabi town, having finished another day of teaching English at the local school. The familiar sound of chirping birds greeted him as he put down his briefcase and hung up his linen jacket in the hallway. He and his partner, Deng, had lived there for five years. They had made short work of the garden that his partner nicknamed the 'little paradise'. It was a favourite place for the butterflies and wildlife and the two men would often sit in the shade, talking and admiring the delicate bloom of white, lilac and purple parrot flowers, so called because of their resemblance to a parrot in flight.

He called to Deng, who answered from the back in the kitchen, asking him if he'd like tea. The phone rang and Raksami picked it up, thinking it was probably the school.

"Hello. Is that Mr Ron?" The voice was flat and spoke to him in English.

"Yes, this is him," he replied with his usual courtesy.

"Ah, excellent," the voice became more friendly. "My name is Mr Lee; I am visiting Krabi and would like to look at a room at the Bird House. I believe it is out of season but I am keen to have a few days' bird watching. Are you available today?"

Mr Ron had started opening his briefcase to search for his diary. "Oh, today? Yes, of course. Are you nearby? I can meet you there in about an hour?"

"Excellent. I shall see you then." The man hung up.

CHAPTER 30

The overnight train journey was quiet and uneventful. There seemed to be very few people travelling. Maria suggested they take advantage of the opportunity to sleep and they both slumped, exhausted, into their bunks. Frank stared at the lights flicking past the window and listened to the rhythmic chug of the tracks.

Jodie's face came into his mind and he wondered what she might be doing at that moment. He remembered a snapshot, one of many, when she would stare at him with her mock pleading, brown eyes; the rest of her face covered by the duvet. It was always a signal to him to get her something, like a cup of tea or toast. Frank would always relent, playfully hitting her with the pillow as he climbed out of the comfortable sanctuary of their bed.

It had been over three months since he'd seen her and he realised that he might not ever see her again. He should have sent a postcard to at least let her know he was alright. They had been together for over four years, after all, and their split had been on good terms. He felt a wave of guilt for not doing so, followed by a moment of sadness. At least he could trust her. Then the terrifying thought came to him of her reading the papers or seeing the news and gasping in shock as he was named as the main suspect for that horrible attack in Asia.

Had the British press picked up the story? Did all his friends currently think he was some kind of secret operative blowing up innocent people for some political agenda?

He made a mental note to ask Carl about the press coverage and drifted into a troubled sleep.

In the morning, the train pulled into Butterworth; across the water lay the island of Penang. They hung around for an hour and then boarded a one carriage train to Hat Yai. Pulling out from the station, Frank saw the wreck of a train on unused tracks that stood like a ghost, a shell of its former self, left to rot and rust. The front engine carriage looked like it had been in some kind of collision. As the train picked up speed, the rooftops of Butterworth changed to fields and dozens of palm trees scattered across the landscape, with the waterway and the island of Penang shimmering in the distance. A wisp of cloud was the only contrast against the wide, deep blue sky.

Ironic. Penang had been somewhere he had planned to visit when he was travelling as a tourist. Now it was passing him by as he fled as a fugitive.

A jovial faced man, sitting opposite, tried to engage Frank and Maria in conversation, but they were both reluctant to talk or give anything away about themselves. Frank closed his eyes and tried to fend off the craving for a cigarette.

In Hat Yai, Frank and Maria hired a Toyota Corolla and they headed north towards Phattalung and then cut across country, west towards Krabi, along the quieter roads of the rural south. On either side, there was an endless sea of palms and fields, interspersed with the occasional dwelling.

Maria glanced at Frank, "Your beard suits you."

Frank scratched at it, "Believe me, it's not out of choice. I can't wait to get rid of it." He paused and let a silence pass before speaking again.

"You never did tell me why you ran off in Goa," he said, eyes fixed on the road.

She looked at him quizzically for a moment and then laughed. "Oh that. I so hate long goodbyes. Why? You think I should have made you breakfast?"

He smiled and stroked her thigh, playfully. "Breakfast would have been icing on the cake."

"I thought it was a one-off thing, at the time," she studied her fingernails. "Besides, you weren't long out of your relationship. I didn't want to be your rebound."

"And then I knocked on your door, a hunted man ... begging for help."

She wrinkled up her nose and laughed. "We'll laugh about it one day."

"We're laughing now, aren't we?" he grinned at her and they both giggled.

After a few miles, Frank glugged at a bottle of water and passed it to Maria. "You handled that chap pretty well, back at your house."

"Yes, I've done a few martial arts classes in my time. It's a handy skill to have."

"Are you a black belt or something?"

"No, nothing that advanced. Just a few classes."

That kind of makes sense, thought Frank as he pressed his foot down on the accelerator and overtook a lorry that had slowed him down.

"It's funny how we managed to overcome him, don't you think? I mean, for an assassin, he seemed pretty unprepared," he said.

Maria gave him a look and frowned. "Yeah, I guess so."

"I mean, if he wanted to kill us he could have easily."

Maria fixed her pale eyes on Frank once again, as if trying to read him and then shrugged. "I've no idea. I'm very glad he didn't though."

He caught sight of Maria's bare leg as she shuffled position in her seat, covered in those light freckles that also adorned her face, and couldn't imagine that she was anyone other than who she claimed to be. Frank let it drop and decided his mind was playing tricks on him.

CHAPTER 31

Frank parked the car a few yards from the entrance to the Bird House and stopped the engine. He turned to Maria.

"Stay here and I'll have a look."

"Let me come with you," she said. He took her hand in his and smiled at her persistence.

"I'd rather you stay here. Please. I won't be long."

Frank walked up the path that had overgrown even more since his first visit that seemed like an age ago. The chirping of the hidden crickets seemed to intensify in the midday heat.

As Frank followed the curve of the pathway he caught a glimpse of Mr Ron's bicycle, propped up against the outside shower room wall. *Good.* That meant he was here and Frank felt a rising optimism. Perhaps he would get some information and answers after all.

Flies spun around chaotically in the air as Frank approached the dilapidated guesthouse. It seemed they were coming from inside the communal area. He peered into the open space to see the familiar sea of palms and overgrowth on the other side, past the veranda set, like a framed painting in the gloom. An old armchair was planted in the middle with its back to him facing the marshland. As Frank's eyes adjusted to the low light, he saw an elbow leaning on the armrest. Mr Ron seemed to be enjoying the view.

"Mr Ron?"

No answer. The buzzing of flies seemed to intensify. Frank suddenly felt something was wrong and he felt his skin go ice cold.

"Mr Ron?" he repeated, more cautiously.

Frank slowly stepped towards the chair. A sickening smell hit the back of his throat, almost making him gag. He clasped his mouth and nose with his hand and inched closer. Now he saw the side of the head and a curious wire that seemed to spring out from his neck. The waxy skinned corpse of Mr Ron sat upright in the chair, buttery fingers grasping the armrest like an alert spider. A thin wire was tightly wrapped around his neck, cutting deep into the throat, and had opened a flow of dark red blood, soaking his chest and stomach through his tropical shirt.

Frank stood transfixed, unable to fully comprehend the sight or move away from the corpse. Mr Ron's eyes stared out across the veranda in frozen terror. Flies crawled over his face, dancing like demons.

"Hello Frank," rasped a low, quiet voice from behind him. Frank spun around, his entire body tense and electrified, heart beating almost out of control.

Half hidden by junk, the figure of Theo slumped on an old sofa, almost in a leisurely pose—had it not been for the dark red spread across his stomach, a violent contrast to his white cotton suit. He clenched the wound, his skin like a pale moon in the shadow, whites of eyes pointed toward Frank, pleadingly.

"Theo? What the hell are you doing here? What happened?"

Frank's eyes stared, disbelievingly, at the familiar face and edged away from the stench of Mr Ron.

"What the hell is going on here?"

Theo somehow managed to grin, despite the intense pain, his handsome face distorting something close to caricature.

"Big gangfuck, Frank. Wouldn't you say?" He coughed and gasped, bile oozing from his mouth; his face sheened with sweat.

Frank swatted a hand at the flies. The air was thick like syrup and he badly wanted to leave, but instead, he stepped towards Theo.

"I'm sorry about Hong Kong, Frank. But you did well ... you're smart." Theo struggled with each word. Frank stopped walking and stared at Theo in disbelief.

"Hong Kong? You were involved in that?"

Theo's eyes rolled and he was near passing out. Frank moved towards him and shook him back to consciousness. "Theo! Who did this?"

"Be careful Frank … he's … psychopathic."

Theo's glazed eyes focused on Frank for the last time, before the life ebbed away from him. Frank shook him again but knew he was dead. He glanced around once more at Mr Ron and slowly moved away from the sofa before turning to run down the pathway as fast as he could.

"Everything OK?" asked Maria, glancing at him with concern.

"Not really," Frank said drily and started the car. "Mr Ron and Theo were in there—both dead. Well, Theo died in front of me. I don't know what the hell is going on. Let's get out of here."

Maria held her hand over her mouth in shock. "Oh God!"

As they drove down towards the town to get onto the main highway, a blue Nissan weaved past them in the opposite direction.

CHAPTER 32

Chiu caught a flash of Frank – at the wheel of the car driving past him – looking like he'd seen a ghost. Chiu didn't think the Englishman had seen him. They must have been at the Bird House and seen his handy work. He had gone down to the town to get supplies, intending to clean up the scene and hide the bodies, but had been delayed for days as he waited for a local contact to get him new equipment. Now, an opportunity had arisen to finish off Frank and the woman. He stopped the car and backed into a driveway to turn around and sped down the hill until he saw the back of their hired white Toyota.

Chiu bitterly regretted not taking them both out back in Hong Kong when he had a chance. Why had he hesitated? He had never flinched when it came to his work before. Stepping into the room, the sight of the woman had thrown him. A thought had come to his mind. He had heard there was a double agent based in Hong Kong but was never privy to the identity of that agent for security reasons. No one was, apart from Oracle. He wondered if his hesitation was because for a split second he had thought it was her?

Or was it because he blanched from killing female targets? He found it hard to do, even if they were the enemy.

Chiu had been brought up by women. His mother and aunt were all he could remember and, as there had been no men around, he became the man of the house. It had helped his self-confidence no end. He fought his peers like a mad dog, never afraid of anyone and he felt aggrieved, angry that his father, who constantly worked away, in a different province to the north, never came back. There were rumours of course. That he had met another woman or had been kidnapped by bandits and his family could not afford to pay. Chiu bore the brunt of constant teasing about it from his school peers which only fuelled his frustration.

Then, he seemed to find solace in one thing—killing. First, it was animals; he would capture a dog or a cat and torture it to death, enjoying that moment as the last flicker of life passed through the animal's eyes. This seemed to calm his inner rage for a short time.

Chiu could not wait to get his P.L.A. army papers, but no opportunities that involved actual kills to satisfy his dark lust seemed to come his way. It was all training, crawling through mud, grappling over walls and roll calls. Only a move to Special Operations Forces would give him what he wanted, what he craved. Or so he thought. In his whole time with the unit, he had only racked up one kill and that was at long range.

Then he was visited by the military intelligence head, Oracle, and his life became dramatically more exciting. His first test: the prisoner in the yard at Nanjing.

And now the Hong Kong clean-up operation was becoming the perfect catalyst for his murderous side. It was what he had been waiting his whole life for.

Chiu lit a cigarette and flicked the ash out of the window, keeping just out of sight from the white Toyota ahead. His thoughts drifted back to Bangkok and the last few weeks. He regretted having to kill Richard the way he did. It was over way too quickly for Chiu's liking. He would have much preferred to have taken him out more slowly but unfortunately, his orders were to make it look like a gangland hit. A shot in the back of the head took less than a second and it seemed like a big anti-climax; there had been a distinct lack of satisfaction.

Then he had the chance to give the Thai police chief the heart attack sermon. Now that had been fun. The wide-eyed fear as he struggled to stop Chiu stabbing the verminous liquid into the police chief's bloodstream and then watching the violent spasms of a full-blown heart attack.

The young man in the shop. A need to try and get information on Bowen's whereabouts had given him the perfect excuse to torture and inflict pain.

And then there was the guesthouse man, Mr Ron, who he had garrotted with piano wire. He claimed to know nothing as he begged for his life but he did say he had put up Frank Bowen. Chiu guessed he probably also had a connection with the criminal, Richard Desmond. Not that it mattered.

It was also unfortunate Theo Kampala had turned up at that moment. He had eventually believed Chiu when he said the victim was an enemy agent. Of course, Theo was his main concern, he needed to be hit, too many loose ends. Despite turning up at the birdhouse, with the same mission to kill Bowen, Kampala had served his purpose.

Yes, despite his doubts about the blonde woman's true identity, he would not hesitate to kill her or the main target now. This had to be wrapped up and quickly.

It had been a roller coaster ride and was just beginning as far as Chiu was concerned. He wouldn't stop now. Once he had disposed of Frank and his girlfriend, he would continue his killing spree. There was no going back.

CHAPTER 33

Lieutenant General Teng of the Special Unit leaned back in his chair, forehead creased with lines and a greying mop of hair hung loosely around his ears. He glanced at the gold watch that his wife had given him and wondered if she'd be offended if he bought himself a new one.

Opposite him sat Chief Inspector Christopher Johnson and Lim Su Sung, his senior inspector of police. There were jugs of water on the table as well as numerous files and papers spread over the surface but there already seemed to be a tension between the two groups.

The inspector read a paper in front of him before meeting Teng with a level stare.

"What we need to know is why Chinese intelligence is trying to kill Frank Bowen."

Teng raised his eyebrows, "Chinese intelligence?"

Inspector Johnson pushed a report across the desk. It was a file on Chiu Won On, his known history, military record and recent C.C.T.V. photographs of the same man in Hong Kong. Teng took it and frowned as he read. "You should have shared this," he said.

"I'm sharing it now. Anyway, this known assassin recently killed a shopkeeper who had helped Frank Bowen get a false passport. He then tracked them to the house of a Maria Amerman Chapman, where they reportedly overpowered him. It's worth pointing out that she is the daughter of Peter Chapman who works for the Legislative Council of Hong Kong.

We received an anonymous call, but he had already escaped. We found fingerprints, so we know he was there."

Teng shrugged, "Yes, we stormed the house before your men got there."

"I know you did, contaminating a crime scene. That, we could have done without," remarked Johnson quietly. Teng frowned, "We were tracking a suspected terrorist for God's sake."

"Reports sent through from MI6 put Frank Bowen and Jimmy Duffy as main suspects for the attack, but they were certainly not working alone. We also had problems confirming these intelligence reports," said Johnson.

Teng said nothing, his face a mask of mild annoyance.

"You had a team at the market very soon after the explosion. You had a tip-off; can you tell us anything about that?" Johnson asked, his eyebrows arched in anticipation.

"I can't reveal anything about our sources, I'm afraid, except that we had reliable information about this operation," Teng snapped.

"And why weren't we told?" interjected Johnson.

Teng slammed his hand down onto the oak table, "We had no time! We had to move a team in fast and even then we were too late to stop the attack," the lieutenant stared hard at the chief inspector, clearly irritated.

Lim Su Sung leaned across and whispered into Johnston's ear. He nodded and turned once again towards Teng. "We'd also like to know the exact source of the reports about the suspects and this tip-off, Lieutenant General."

Teng waved a dismissive hand, his voice raised. "I cannot tell you that right now, maybe in time. But we have a job to do and that is tracking these terrorists and protecting Hong Kong."

"Yes and we have to do our job," retorted Johnson, "We need to find out what the hell is going on. There could be more attacks if Chinese intelligence is behind this and it looks like they are trying to frame MI6 for carrying out a false flag operation. We need your co-operation, Lieutenant."

Teng breathed heavily as if trying to hold in his temper.

"Of course we will co-operate, Chief Inspector."

"Then tell me the source!"

Teng paused and stared down at the table, "MI6," he said.

Johnson frowned, "So they knew about the attack beforehand? They told you and you went to the locations? Why weren't—" He stopped himself, frustrated.

Teng shuffled in his seat. "I'll level with you. The message was to keep your boys out of it, initially anyway. As I said, we were given very little time."

Johnson felt even more confused and he had several questions in his head. But he only asked one more, "Can you give the exact MI6 codename of the source?"

"There was no information on where it came from exactly. It was anonymously delivered."

Johnson and Su Sung glanced at each other. "Alright. Thanks for your help, Mr Teng." Chairs scraped as the meeting ended.

CHAPTER 34

"Yes, Governor Wilson, I'll keep you informed. Goodbye." The chief inspector put the phone down and glanced up at Lim Su Song, senior inspector of police.

"The Governor's anxious about the investigation. Is the detective inspector ready?" asked Johnson.

"Yes, he's already in the situation room," answered the senior inspector.

Johnson and Lim Su Sung walked into the long, bright room where Detective Inspector Brown was tinkering around with the window blinds to block out the fierce sunlight. A board on the wall had photographs, maps and notes pinned all over it, resembling a puzzle. Johnson and Lim Su Song sat down at the large table that dominated the room and slapped down their files.

The detective inspector cleared his throat, "I'll start with what we know so far."

"One bomb detonated on the number 61 tram at Chun Yeung Street market at 10.45am on the 2nd February. Then the 11.30am MTR train to Causeway Bay blew up as it entered the station at 11.37am, causing seventeen deaths and multiple injuries." Inspector Brown gestured to photographs of the immediate aftermath on the wall. He then produced the same passport photograph of Jimmy Duffy that had appeared on the news from a briefcase on the table in front of him.

"This man, who we had identified as Jimmy Duffy from Northern Ireland, was shot dead by the Special Unit at the street market immediately after the explosion. They had apparently been tipped off about the attack and were at the scene minutes after the explosion. We're still trying to find out where this tip-off came from. According to his file, he has Ulster Defence Association connections, but we're treating that with a big pinch of salt."

Brown moved to the other side of the board and pointed out Frank Bowen's passport photograph.

"Frank Bowen ... who is still at large and could be linked to the Causeway Bay attack. He arrived in Hong Kong on the same flight as Jimmy Duffy and they split up at the airport."

"This is where it gets interesting. Frank Bowen's fingerprints have been placed at the scene of the murder of Li Wu, who was a passport forger. There were also fingerprints of Chiu Wah On, an operative of MSS and former People's Army. We believe him to be operating for a division within Chinese intelligence. Witnesses also have placed a man of his description entering Li's shop before the time of death."

Brown paused and sipped his water before continuing. "An anonymous call, which was traced to Malaysia, tipped us off about an intruder in the home of this woman, Maria Amerman Chapman. Apparently, the intruder had been tied up, but we only found cut rope and signs of a struggle. No sign of Maria Chapman. We did, however, find fingerprints, from both Frank Bowen and our friend, Chiu Wah On.

Right now I'm coordinating a concerted effort to track down Frank Bowen and Maria Chapman. Frank Bowen is most certainly travelling on a false passport. We already had the airport security unit and all exit control points notified, but we can't rule out that he's already left Hong Kong."

Detective Brown paused and looked up at the two men sat in front of him. "Any questions so far?"

Johnson gestured for him to continue.

"So, we need to find these two suspects as soon as possible. Also, I've asked the sergeant to question her father; see if that brings anything up."

Lim Su Song shifted his weight in his chair, "It might be an idea to go through all their background files again to see if we may have missed something—an alternative to our current source if possible. It would be good to have a second opinion."

Johnson chimed in, "The two men, Bowen and Duffy. They came in from Bangkok, what's the track on their movements?"

"Our line of enquiry with the Bangkok police has revealed they stayed in a guesthouse on Khao San Road. I'll put a full list in the report."

Johnson clicked his pen, flipping it round and round in his hand. "Do we have any idea where the explosives came from?"

Brown sighed, "Not at the moment. It's much too early to tell. Forensics is still going through the crime scenes."

Johnson thought for a moment and then opened his file for the first time, almost hesitating. "Well, the location of the MI6 station that supplied the false Intel to the Special Unit came through and it's pretty worrying, to say the least."

He handed the sheet to Detective Brown, whose eyes quickly fell on the paper and widened as he saw that it was the station right there in their own city; the Hong Kong station.

CHAPTER 35

Frank found a phone and dialled the same number he had before, pouring Baht coins into the slot. It took a while; several redials later, Frank heard Carl's voice.

"Frank, good to hear you. There's nothing on a Dean Whiteman, no one with a record anyway. I have some other news though. Your friend Richard Desmond is dead. He was found in his apartment, classic execution style. He was just a lowlife villain, but a connected one, doing anything for the highest bidder. He also had a record in the UK, petty stuff, drug trafficking."

Frank took in the words as he watched a dog lying flat on its side, sleeping on the shaded platform as though it were dead. "He was assassinated?"

"Yep. Right or wrong, he's out of the picture."

"Jesus!" Frank paused before continuing: "Listen, I've got another name for you. Theo Kampala. I met him in Goa but I found him in Krabi with a dead guesthouse owner. He admitted involvement and then died before I could get anything more out of him. He'd been shot and the other guy had been throttled with piano wire."

"That doesn't sound good."

"What the hell is going on? Why are they doing this, Carl?"

"Frank, it's pretty complicated from what I can see. We've got the Hong Kong authorities screaming the same questions. It looks like a False Flag op. Basically the Chinese have set this up and tried to make it look like a MI6 gig. There are stories in the Chinese press that it's a Brit operation and the authorities are sticking to that story and accusing us of murdering Hong Kong citizens. To what end I do not know. You should get the hell out of there and come home."

"And get locked up for God knows how long? You know as well as I do that I'm still blamed by the Hong Kong authorities and probably by your lot, officially anyway. Maybe not by you personally, Carl, but I don't trust anyone at the moment."

"Look, I'm trying to find out all I can. Hong Kong Police did contact us trying to verify a report we allegedly sent them. It claimed you were connected to us as well as a few terrorist organisations."

"What?"

"It came from Hong Kong, not here. But Frank, listen, we'll sort this out, don't worry."

Frank fell silent as the line crackled badly for a few seconds before returning to normal. He was about to say something and then thought better of it as a thought crossed his mind.

"You OK, Frank? Hello?"

"Yes, Carl, I'm still here. Listen, what is the British press saying? Please tell me my photo isn't plastered all over the bloody Sun newspaper?"

"No, we buried it. There was a small piece in the Times but it's hardly made the news. Everyone's attention is on the Gulf war."

Frank sighed in relief. "OK, I'll call you later, Carl. Thanks for your help mate." He put down the phone and walked back to where Maria was waiting outside Surat Thani train station.

"Is everything OK?" she asked.

Frank forced a smile but his mind was still taking in what Carl had said. "My friend gave me some background but the Bangkok situation has changed slightly. Want to get a drink?"

Frank wondered for a moment if the report Carl had mentioned had been doctored by someone in London, not Hong Kong. Had he been involved somehow and was now attempting to cover his tracks by telling him?

Now that Richard was dead and God knows who else, there was no reason to go to Bangkok, except, of course, to get the money he'd stashed there. But going to the Thai capital now seemed too dangerous.

"Frank?" Maria studied him, her hand touching his as they sat in a café near the train station. He shook his head and smiled. "Sorry, I'm miles away."

His face went serious. "Maria. The guy I wanted to get some answers from in Bangkok is dead. I think you're right. Going there was never a good idea."

She looked at him, shocked, and then asked how. Frank told her and she looked relieved that he had scrapped that plan.

"I think I need to lie low for a while. I read about a great place. It means a train back South again, I'm afraid, and possibly a boat. If you're game, that is?"

"Well, well. You are the dark horse, Mr Bowen." She gave him a full smile, the one he could never resist.

Neither of them noticed the blue Nissan parked opposite.

CHAPTER 36

Ho Zhang looked out across the Beijing skyline; the grey smog settled leaving only vague shapes of buildings visible as if it were a painting. He suspected that he might be seeing the view for the last time and put on his jacket before checking himself in the mirror. He then made his way down in the lift, stepping out into the humidity, and told his driver to take him to the headquarters of the Ministry of State Security.

Zhang stepped warily up the polished steps to the building and entered the vast lobby area that echoed his footsteps up to the ceiling. He reported his appointment and verified his identification before sitting down on a long bench. After half an hour of waiting, a guard walked over, dressed in immaculate uniform, and asked him to accompany him to the lift.

On the top floor, Zhang waited another fifteen minutes before being called into the office. He bowed and sat down nervously in front of Xu Yun, the agency head, who nodded as he finished off writing on a notepad in front of him. Yun had a bullish red face and large bags under his eyes. A reflection of nearly fifty years in the intelligence service, thought Zhang as he glanced over the framed certificates on the wall behind him. There was a photograph of a much younger Yun shaking the hands of a man that he did not recognise.

Yun stood up and Zhang quickly followed his lead and they shook hands.

"Thanks for coming, Ho Zhang," he said gruffly and pulled a folder out that was set aside, opening it to reveal Zhang's file.

"So," he began, "Mr Zhang. A graduate of The University

of International Affairs?" Zhang nodded in agreement. He had enrolled at the University in 1979 which had re-opened a year earlier, following a hiatus due to the Cultural Revolution. The University had been brought under the control of the Ministry of Public Security in 1965 and was charged with training intelligence agents for the Investigation Department, which later became the Ministry of State Security.

"And you seemed to be in the right place at the right time when the National People's Congress established the Ministry of State Security under the State Council?" Yun looked up and peered at him from under a pair of thick eyebrows.

"Yes, you could put it like that, yes." The MSS had indeed been established out of the old intelligence service, the Central Investigation Department of the Ministry of Public Security under Deng Xiaoping, perceiving a growing threat of subversion and sabotage.

Yun flipped the pages and came to one that he stared at momentarily before shutting the folder entirely and leaning back in his chair.

"The operations your department have been carrying out are, I'm sure, all in the interest of our great country. I've been receiving your reports. The Hong Kong situation..." The old man paused as if reluctant to mention details, "Is it under control?"

Zhang cleared his throat. He had prepared for this.

"Everything went according to our wishes, it was very smooth, Sir. The operation took two years to plan and we anticipated most things. We did have a slight problem in that one of the terrorists escaped the theatre of operation. I, therefore, sent our agent Tian to take care of it. This is still in progress and I have no doubt this will be concluded very soon," Zhang paused, unsure whether to carry on. The shadows under Yun's eyes seemed to darken and he leaned forward.

"We have had to respond to the changes in this operation. Denying it all, of course, and our press agencies have pointed fingers at the British, but if any of this gets out it will be severely damaging, you understand? Your plan to use Orchid to lay the trail to MI6 was a good one. But it seems to be unravelling, is it not?"

"Sir. The only problem is the terrorist, which we're on top of, I assure you."

Yun suddenly grabbed a Bangkok Post newspaper and threw it onto the desk in front of Zhang, jabbing his finger at a prominent story on two bodies found in Krabi.

"There are bodies piling up all over Asia. Your agent is cleaning up a little too publicly!"

Zhang bowed his head. "It won't happen again. I will send orders..."

"No, it will not happen again because you're going to shut down all operations as of now. The department is closed until further notice." Yun's face seemed to become almost as red as the Chinese flag on the wall.

Then, as quickly as he had exploded in anger, the old man seemed to calm again, "The State Council is concerned and asking questions. It's put me in a very tricky situation. I have no choice. Don't worry, you will not be arrested. You will be reassigned."

Zhang held his eyes shut for a moment and nodded. He began talking slowly and quietly: "Most of the agents I can recall. As I'm sure you're aware, agent Orchid is a quality product who delivers us very useful information from within MI6. How do you suggest I handle it?"

"I know losing such a valuable asset is not easy to take, Zhang, but they are going to be compromised sooner or later. Cut the agent loose."

CHAPTER 37

The curtains opened and Frank could make out the outline of Maria's hair in the gloom.

She climbed into the cramped space, astride Frank, finding a comfortable spot that suited them both. Their lips met and soon their bodies were intertwined in a quiet urgency. No words. Just a need to be close.

Yet the uncertainty of who she really was floated at the back of Frank's mind as they made love, both fighting to keep their gasps quiet.

Could she really be some kind of honey trap? Right then he almost didn't care.

As they lay together, letting the rhythm of the train envelop them, Maria gently stroked a loose wisp of Frank's hair back into place.

"Do you think if we get out of this there'll be something for us on the other side?" she whispered.

Frank smiled, moving his hand up and down her bare back.

"I'm sure there'll be a lot for us if we want there to be." He realised for the first time the risk she was taking by coming with him. She could just have easily stayed well out of it and pointed him on his way.

"Thanks for being with me," he said.

Frank's body absorbed the gentle rumble of the train carriages that vibrated the bunk bed. He wanted to drift off to sleep but he realised, with irritation, that nature called.

Untangling himself from Maria, he pulled on his shorts,

slipped into flip-flops and made his way down the quiet, dimly lit train.

He had to pass through an empty catering carriage and then another sleeping car before finding a toilet. He closed and locked the door to the cramped cubicle, splashing cold water over his face from the running tap. Staring at himself in the mirror, he wondered when he was going to be able to shave off the bloody beard. Frank hated it. He then proceeded to take a leak.

A moment later, he opened the door to come back out and caught sight of a Chinese man passing by. He seemed familiar, even from behind, and Frank could see the edge of his scar. The intruder in Hong Kong! Amazingly, he hadn't noticed Frank, but it was definitely the same man. He knew it. Frank thought fast, realising that this guy was probably looking to quietly kill them in their sleep.

How the hell did he find them? Was it coincidence? No, it couldn't possibly be.

Frank stepped out of his flip flops and crouched low, waiting for his moment, whilst frantically looking around for some kind of weapon. The Chinese wasn't looking in the sleeping berths, instead walking purposefully along the narrow corridor, reading the berth numbers, obviously knowing where they were sleeping. The assassin approached the catering carriage, sliding the door to go through. Frank had to act soon. If the intruder had looked around behind him at that moment, he would have seen Frank stalking after him in nothing but his shorts but the Chinese continued through the sliding doors. Frank just managed to catch the door with his hand before it slammed shut and slipped through, immediately spotting a fire extinguisher placed just inside the carriage.

Struggling to release it from its grip Frank glanced up and saw that the killer was halfway through the catering carriage and would soon reach his and Maria's beds. He wobbled the whole of the canister to free it from its bearings but age seemed to have welded it in place as it stubbornly refused to budge.

Finally, with one final effort using all his body weight, it came free in his hands, almost throwing him off balance. He moved fast, running down towards the end of the carriage to build the momentum of speed, as the killer approached the doorway. The noise of the train hid the sound of his footfall. As Frank got to within three metres of him, Chiu started to turn around as if he sensed the movement approaching.

Frank threw the fire extinguisher at him with all his force. The Chinese instinctively dodged the canister but it still bounced off the side of his head, ricocheting off the plastic carriage door back onto his neck, throwing him forward onto his knees. Frank used the momentum of his speed to shove him over again with his foot, stubbing his toes on the man's shoulder.

Ignoring the shot of pain, Frank went to grab the fire extinguisher again but the killer adopted a defensive stance, kicking the inside of his knee. Frank fell back onto the ground, yelling in agony. Jabbing violently at Chiu with his feet; he tried to crawl backwards, the adrenaline pumping hard in his veins. The assassin attempted to pull himself to his feet by using the side of a table to lever himself while rolling back the canister out of Frank's reach with his foot.

Then Frank saw a chilli pot on the table and grabbed it, immediately throwing the powder at Chiu's eyes with a swoop of his arm. The man cursed in Mandarin, holding up his hands to his face as Frank followed up with a full kick onto his chest to force him back down against the carriage door.

Frank had to prevent the assassin from getting near him as he had seen first-hand, at Krabi, what he was capable of. He went to kick again and this time the killer grabbed his leg, twisting it at the same time, making Frank yell out in agony as he was pulled down to the floor. Chiu managed to lunge forward, throwing himself onto Frank, one hand grabbing his neck while the right hand came around, holding a syringe, pointing it directly at Frank's chest. Frank grabbed the arm holding the syringe, to prevent getting jabbed. The two men's faces were inches apart, Chiu's bloodshot eyes glaring at Frank with pure hatred; teeth bared as saliva dripped onto Frank's neck. Frank used all his strength to prevent the needle going into him—if that happened he knew he was dead.

Frank shouted for help. No one could hear above the chugging tracks and, besides, the doors both ends were shut. He was strong, but the Chinese seemed stronger and the needle inched closer. He felt his strength ebb as the hand gripping his throat seemed to close up his windpipe, draining him of air.

At that moment, a pair of hands appeared low down through the sliding door to grab the canister from the ground. Frank saw it was Maria and jerked his head; butting the killer's face with his forehead to distract him.

Maria held the fire extinguisher above her and brought it down at the back of the assassin's skull with all the force she could conjure. There was a sickening crack and Chiu's head slumped against Frank's shoulder, blood streaming from his wound.

Frank pushed the limp hand away from his throat, coughing and wheezing, spitting drool out of his mouth. Maria helped pull the lifeless body slumped on top of Frank aside. Frank managed to get free and crawled onto his hands and knees, coughing thick bile onto the ground. It was several minutes before he could speak.

"Thanks, Maria. This is becoming a habit," he rasped, voice almost gone as he somehow managed to flash her a grin.

"Can we get out of here?" she asked urgently.

"What about him? You think … he's still alive?" asked Frank. They both looked at the still unconscious body.

"Not sure." Maria leaned down and held his pulse for a moment. "Yes, just."

"Let's get rid of him, out the door," said Frank, slowly pulling himself to his feet.

"Throw him out of the door? That would definitely kill him, Frank."

"He was trying to kill me. This is the second time he's caught up with us. No more chances," Frank said, a look of grim determination on his face. Then he looked at the syringe gripped in Chiu's hand and eased it free, holding it up to the flicking carriage light to study the liquid content.

"God knows what this is. Maybe I could give him a dose of his own medicine?"

"We haven't got time for this!" Maria was looking back

through the inner door window into their carriage, clearly worried.

"OK, let's do it. All clear?" asked Frank as he began to drag Chiu towards the door. Maria went through into the carriage and used all her strength to push open the main door which buttressed against the force of outside air that rushed by. The door swept back, banging against the carriage metal, and she quickly stepped back to allow Frank to drag Chiu to the doorframe.

A moment later, the body had disappeared into the inky night, along with the syringe and Frank pulled the door closed. He rested against it for a moment before gesturing to Maria. "We'd better clean up and get off this train."

CHAPTER 38

Douglas Brown pressed the buttons on the vending machine and watched his coffee cup drop down onto the tray and fill with black liquid, quickly followed by white, frothy milk. He grabbed it, winced as he burned his fingers and walked back to his desk where another pile of paperwork had magically appeared. The detective inspector cleaned his glasses on his shirt and blew the top of the coffee in an attempt to cool it down. The first report was from the forensics at the scene of the explosion in Causeway Bay.

He read for two minutes then jumped out of his seat, walking briskly to the chief inspector's office and knocked rapidly before poking his head around the door.

"Chief?"

Johnson nodded, gesturing for him to come in.

"Report from forensics. The explosion at Causeway Bay was caused by a device underneath the train, not inside the carriage. The force of it ripped up through the floor." He paused and handed over the report. "I actually saw that myself, but it didn't register at the time."

"Anything from the tram attack?"

"There's nothing in yet," Brown replied. "I have a feeling it will be the same."

Johnson leaned forward. "Douglas. Find Frank Bowen. We need to talk to him. Tell him he's in the clear, but on the condition, he comes back to Hong Kong from wherever he's hiding. I'll make a call to MI6. It's time we compared notes."

CHAPTER 39

A row of clocks in various time zones on the pale, flaking wall had faithfully displayed the time for over twenty years. Mary Lo didn't hold much love for the windowless room that sat in the centre of the MI6 Hong Kong station but was thankful she was able to lose herself in her work to block it out at least.

She ran her eyes down the Personals advert column of the Hong Kong Times once again. It was a painstaking task to which she had devoted a few hours a day, unless she saw a lead and then she'd be off like a dog with a bone, working through the entire evening. The word 'orchid' written into one of the ads seemed to stand out, turning tiny cogs in her brain. It was one of the keywords on her list; words that cropped up that may have significant meaning and even be part of a message.

Having the job of checking the Personals column had, of course, drawn plenty of comments from her male colleagues. "You're secretly looking for Mr Right, eh Mary?"

"Yeah, no real men around here," she'd usually fire back.

Mary walked over to a filing cabinet and flipped through previous issues that she had marked and catalogued. She found the page that she was looking for and looked over one of the ads again, spreading it open over a nearby table.

"To my loving K. My flame is growing every day. Miss You – Orchid."

Another said:

"My darling K, I could not share you with another. If our love is to grow I must have a reply. Orchid."

She started to follow the trail and look for possible responses to the message in editions a day or so afterwards, messages that would consistently fit and look as if they were connected. She couldn't initially see any obvious culprits, but then that was the idea with hidden messages.

Mary went through the ads one by one and wrote down each letter, matching them to common code encryptions until she had a group of numbers in rows. She ran through the numbers in Chinese dialects – Mandarin, locally known as Guoyu, Cantonese, Hakka, Yin – as well as English. It was a thinking process more than anything. One which took time. Plenty of time.

Messages could be transmitted in a variety of ways, depending on the circumstances. They could be via the World Wide Web, a technology that was increasingly being used by universities, groups and enthusiasts. Then there were various levels of Cryptography. The Data Encryption Standard (DES) and the Advanced Encryption Standard (AES) were block cypher designs which had been set as cryptography standards by the US government but were unlikely to be used by Chinese intelligence.

Mary mainly focused on 'In Plain Sight' messages where the mailbox was public, such as newspapers and magazines, even radio messages. Benjamin Fowler, an intelligence officer based at the Hong Kong station for over twelve years, entered the room and nodded at Mary.

"How's the world of Miss Lo? Breaking those codes?" he smiled. His short, cropped, blond hair seemed to get lighter by the year, Mary thought.

"Oh yes. Firing through it, almost done," she joked, sarcastically. She glanced down at her notes as if pondering something. "There is something."

She explained her hunch about the personals as she flipped through the papers pointing out the marked suspect adverts.

"Orchid huh? I'll throw it at matey boy downstairs and see if it shakes any leaves," Fowler said, his eyes scanning over the newsprint. "You never know."

Fowler left Mary to her notes to fetch his colleague and question their suspect. The pressure had been building on him and he was acutely aware he needed answers, especially one that dug deep into his psyche and had kept him awake in recent weeks.

He remembered getting wind of the fake report naming Frank Bowen and Jimmy Duffy as terrorists that had been supplied to the Special Unit purporting to come from MI6. Worse, it had since come to light that it had come from his station. Finding the agent responsible, from the twenty or so operating in the area, was proving to be more difficult than he had anticipated, especially with the evasive experience they all had.

Fowler opened the door to the room and nodded at the large, burly man studying a wall map inside.

"Ready, Grant?"

The man grunted and followed Fowler back out into the corridor. They descended metal steps down several floors, lit only by faded bulbs set into the hard walls.

****

Underground, in the anonymous concrete building, a Chinese man paced around a clammy, windowless room, relief brought only when the ceiling fan kicked in for around five minutes every half hour. Aside from a simple fold-out bed and a solitary table, there was nothing in the claustrophobic space. He unconsciously ran a hand across the bruising on his cheek and then massaged the back of his neck, trying to guess the time. He thought it might be the afternoon, but was unsure. He reckoned this was his third day or so of captivity with very little sleep. The fluorescent tube of light that stretched across the ceiling stayed on permanently. It was a shame the fan didn't stay on, he thought. Both these technical hitches were obviously deliberate.

He thought back to the night his captors wanted to know more about. Three months as a security guard – sitting in that booth every night and watching hours of crap on T.V. – and then the night his comrades came and the three figures had walked down the platform.

Where it came to an end at the tunnel, the three men took out torches from their bags and jumped down onto the rail track and Heng handed them down the heavy bags, one by one, grunting at the weight of them.

The scar-faced one had looked up at him as the other two slowly moved off into the darkness of the tunnel, their torch lights dancing around the tracks.

"The model number?"

Heng had nodded and taken a piece of paper out of his inside jacket pocket, quickly checking it again before handing it over. Scarface looked at it: "This is definitely the right one?"

Heng met the dark eyes and jerked his head confidently. "Definitely."

"Ok, good work. Stay here and guard." And then he had disappeared into the blackness.

The thick iron door to the room rattled with the sounds of keys struggling with the lock before the imposing figure of Grant appeared, filling the door frame.

"Time for a tea break, mate," he said and the Chinese man voluntarily held out his wrists which Grant quickly clasped in handcuffs. They walked a short distance along a dank corridor that had never seen a shred of daylight and entered another windowless room where Benjamin Fowler was opening a metallic briefcase. He hooked leads from the Ambassador Polygraph machine that was housed in the case to an external monitor sitting on a table next to him. The Chinese man held out his hands again, letting Fowler release his cuffs, before sitting down in the same chair he had sat in four times previously. Before that, he had been kidnapped by masked figures, blindfolded and brought to this shithole.

The big man wrapped a black blood pressure armband around his left bicep and attached two monitor devices to his chest.

Fowler glanced at Grant, "Ready to rock and roll?"

Grant gave the devices attached to the Chinese man one more glance, "Yes, go ahead."

"I want to see my lawyer," said the suspect, giving the two intelligence officers a steady glare.

"Fuck your lawyer," smiled Grant. "With respect," he added. The Chinese exhaled slowly, it was the same answer he'd received in the previous four times of asking.

The questions began with the regular familiarity. What is your name? Where do you live? Did you place the bombs at Causeway Bay or Chun Yeung Street market?

The Chinese had not answered anything and had refused to speak, however, he was beginning to deny some of the questions, which the polygraph machine seemed okay with. Grant chain-smoked as he ran through the routine questions and felt a rising sense of frustration, even though he knew that this was a long ball game. There had been many deaths on their turf and there was still a distinct lack of progress as far as the public was concerned, although the finger had very much swung in the direction of Beijing.

"Who planted the bombs?"

"I don't know anything about the bombs," he said quietly. Fowler glanced at the monitor line, which remained steady.

"Did you plant the bombs?"

The Chinese man, Mu Heng, who had not revealed his name, kept his eyes on the wall behind his interrogator and his breathing and heart beat had remained steady. Beating a polygraph machine wasn't easy, there was a distinct method. Polygraph examinations looked for significant involuntary responses in a person's body when they were subjected to stress. Stress associated with deception.

"Who is Orchid?"

Mu Heng blinked quickly. He knew of Orchid. He shouldn't have been aware of that codename, but he had heard stories from fellow operatives. Something about that question had surprised him and Fowler noted – with satisfaction – that the monitor line darted erratically up and down.

Both men made their way back upstairs to the main operations room and studied the monitor print-out.

"He's definitely lying or hiding something," Fowler said.

"Yes, I know he's involved in the bombing, you know he's involved. But why does nothing show up in the graphs for that line of questioning?" asked Grant, clearly not satisfied.

"He wasn't expecting us to ask about Orchid though. He was expecting the bomb questions and has been ready for them from the beginning, but this clearly threw him. Maybe he's not specifically trained for long-term interrogation. We've had him for four days. Maybe the lack of sleep is kicking in?"

Fowler saw that Grant looked unconvinced. "Don't worry about it. This is good. Orchid could be the link."

From briefings with the Hong Kong police and the Special Unit, Fowler had begun to string together what they were dealing with. The prisoner had worked as a watchman at the train terminal for just over a year, where all the trains on the island were serviced, refuelled and checked. After a tip-off, he had been taken by officers of the MI6 Hong Kong station before the police could get him. He had traces of explosives on his hands. At his address, they found bomb-making equipment as well as a whole pile of other evidence. In Fowler's mind, he was guilty as surely as the sun rose in the morning. It was the network behind the watchman Fowler needed to break. As soon as possible.

The phone rang and Grant took it before handing it over to Fowler. He listened to the voice for several moments and uttered a thank you before putting down the phone.

"Cody hasn't turned up to his job again."

Cody was a codename for one of their agents who had been missing and uncontactable for several days, and it was beginning to seriously concern Fowler.

CHAPTER 40

Frank and Maria sat on the top deck of the aqua green painted ferry that transported locals and the odd traveller from Parapat across to Samosir Island, a volcanic landmass that sat in the middle of Lake Toba in Sumatra. The air was fresh at this higher level and clouds hung low, obscuring parts of the mountains in the distance. They disembarked at a small drop off point that consisted of a wooden platform and walked to the reception and restaurant area that rented out traditional Batak houses that sat alongside the lakes.

The proprietor was a short, stocky Indonesian with a jovial face that reminded Frank of the British comedian Benny Hill. "For you, I have lovely Batak house just available," he had said with unbridled enthusiasm and charm. He had led them back down to the lake, ushering them into one of the beautifully painted Batak houses at the end of a row. It stood so close to the lake that it was possible to dive in right from the door. Frank and Maria decided to take it straight away and settled in, unpacking their bags before sitting outside on two fold up wooden chairs to take in the scenery.

Sunlight skimmed across the surface of the water, the only sound seemed to be the squeak of a water pump some distance behind them.

"I spoke to my father, rang him from the station in K.L.," Maria said suddenly, staring out at the lake, "I just wanted to check he was alright with everything that was going on. I'm sorry, I should have told you. He said he loved me very much," she looked at Frank, her eyes wide and glistening.

Frank nodded, remembering his suspicions. "I'm glad he does love you Maria, wouldn't be much of a father if he didn't."

"I know, but you don't understand. He has never told me that in my entire life," she said. Her face seemed etched with questions.

"Oh? Well, maybe he thought it was overdue? He was worried about you," Frank offered.

Maria shook her head in disagreement. It had played on her mind directly after the phone call, but she had pushed it to the back of her consciousness. She felt now, more than ever, something was wrong.

After a few days, they took the highly recommended walk to a village a few miles up the road. As the road climbed higher into the hills, they admired the breathtaking view of the rice fields stretching into the distance that resembled a patchwork quilt.

When they returned to the restaurant, the owner beckoned Frank over and Maria went ahead to the house. Frank had asked that he let him know if anyone came snooping around.

"Man with grey hair, English man. He ask for you. He not stay here, came after you left," he said, excitedly.

"Did he say who he was?" He had not.

Several hours later, Frank sat outside the Batak house and watched a figure walk towards him. He wore a black shirt – that was in a military style, with shoulder lapels and two pockets across the front – and white slacks. His hair was grey, swept back, and he wore black-rimmed glasses. Frank guessed he was in his mid-forties. The man nodded at Frank as he approached and then stopped in front of him.

"Frank Bowen?" Frank froze and narrowed his eyes. "I'm Douglas Brown, detective inspector at the Royal Hong Kong police force. Don't worry, I'm here unofficially. I just want to talk."

"I don't suppose you have I.D. to prove that, do you?"

"Yes, of course." He fished out his wallet and flipped it open, revealing the badge. He held it towards Frank to give him a clear view.

"Something you bought in Bangkok?" Frank asked, eyebrows arched. The inspector laughed out loud. "Well I know you can pretty much buy anything there nowadays but, no, it is genuine, trust me." Frank decided to do just that. Trust him. He wasn't in a position to do anything else and, besides, he hoped this inspector had some answers.

"How did you find me?" asked Frank.

"Indonesian customs reported it. There were no arrest warrants in place but we wanted notification. I've spent quite a while tracking you down. Have to admit it's been an interesting experience, running around Sumatra after your tail. It wasn't that difficult though," he smiled, a look of satisfaction on his face.

They sat at the water's edge, on a makeshift wooden platform that acted as a diving point to the Lake. The inspector dangled his feet over the edge, hovering just above the water.

"It's a beautiful spot," he said, gazing over towards the far mountains. A cloud of mist hung, obscuring the far side.

"It certainly is. Quiet and peaceful, something I've been badly in need of recently," said Frank, a hint of regret in his voice as if he'd been sloppy in covering his tracks.

Brown looked at him and smiled. "Yes, I can sympathise with you there," he said.

Frank leaned forward, turning to face the man from Hong Kong, "What happened to me exactly, inspector? I've got my theories, but I'm dying to hear yours," he said.

"Off the record," he paused to take a gulp of beer that Frank had brought from the house, "You were set up, we know that now."

Frank laughed, "Yeah, that's one thing I do know."

"Some element in MSS decided to carry out a false flag operation. By launching attacks, they made Hong Kong look weak and incapable when it came to their own security. Among other reasons it was to give the Chinese an upper hand in the takeover negotiations."

"Jesus, that's crazy," Frank almost spat in the water.

"Maybe, but hardly surprising," said Brown. "Emperors, governments and intelligence agencies all have a long history in false flag operations, including our own. In fact, we pretty much pioneered it. A British Army Officer, Frank Kitson, wrote a book on it: 'Low-Intensity Operations – Subversion Insurgency & Peacekeeping.' He wrote that if there's an organisation or group and you want to discredit them, you create your own parallel organisation. You send them out to commit atrocities which will be blamed on the original relatively benign group, and they'll be discredited, demonised, and you gain political advantage. It's on my bookshelf at home."

"Intelligence agencies, Governments and their power plays," said Frank quietly.

"What I don't understand is Richard Desmond's involvement. He's just a criminal, no intelligence links that we know of," Brown said.

"I think I can help you there," said Frank, peeling off the beer bottle label. "I met someone calling himself Theo Kampala in Goa. He suggested I go to this guesthouse in Bangkok, which I did, and that's where I met Richard Desmond. Theo turned up in Krabi and admitted his involvement before he died. That's all I know."

Brown nodded slowly. "Yes, I saw a report on that. Theo's real name is, or was, Amith Kumar and he worked for Chinese intelligence as a scout based in India. From what we know, it seems his job was to pick suitable patsies—Western travellers with few, or no, family connections. He put you in touch with Desmond and fed your information, as well as Jimmy's, back to the Beijing station."

Frank shook his head.

"I'm sorry, Frank, you were pretty unlucky."

Frank managed a laugh and took a swig of beer.

"So, by putting out false information on you and your friend, making out you were connected to MI6 and so forth, they created a story, an illusion," Brown continued. "Rogue operatives, backed by British intelligence or a terrorist group, whose plan was to plant the timed explosives on public transport—except, in your case, you were to go up with it. The story would be it was an accident and that you hadn't timed it right."

"So they weren't going to paint us as some kind of kamikaze suicide bombers?"

Brown sighed, adjusting his spectacles. "I don't think so, but I could be wrong. We'll never know, probably. The big picture is that it was all to deflect attention away from the Chinese. But you survived. You should have been blown to pieces on that train, but by missing it they had to find you. It seems to me, once they tried to clean up the loose ends, things went from bad to worse for them. The main culprit was their agent: Tian. The one hunting you."

"Yeah, what a bloody psycho he was!"

The inspector glanced at Frank. "His body was found beside a train track near Alor Satar. So he's out of the picture, you'll be pleased to know."

Frank smiled thinly, his heart racing as he forced himself to keep a calm exterior.

"That's great news to me, Douglas," he said, a little too loudly. Brown looked at him quizzically for a moment, before looking back across the lake at another brightly painted ferry coming in from the mainland.

"Someone at MI6 was responsible for setting you up, you realise that, Frank?" Brown's tone was deadly serious again. Frank frowned at the inspector.

"The reports we received about you and Jimmy, as well as the tip-offs about the exact location and time of the attacks, all came from within MI6."

"Shit!" Frank's head slumped downwards, his eyes staring at his own reflection in the dark water.

"The exact agent source was unidentifiable. We double checked officially and an intelligence officer confirmed that the information sent was not bona fide. Essentially, it was false information."

Frank jerked his head to face the inspector, "Who?"

"We don't know. But it's got to be a mole. There has to be a Chinese agent deep within their organisation."

CHAPTER 41

Orchid picked up the phone and thought he heard a click but wasn't sure. Replacing it back in the cradle, he moved to the window, which was covered by a closed blind, and peeked through it, out of habit more than anything. He paced around the back room, churning the situation over in his mind. It wasn't good.

There had been no response from Oracle to his last three messages. Even if he had to bail out, he wanted assurances that he could defect back to the nest, but none was forthcoming.

Keep calm, he told himself, but deep down he knew it was only a matter of time before he was uncovered.

He had done everything they had required and more and this is how they repaid years of service? He had filed constant reports right up to informing them where to find Frank Bowen's passport contact.

The obvious way was to disappear and yet there was a loose end that he could not ignore, one that pulled at his stomach, tying it into knots, making him feel sick.

The tall man slumped down in an armchair, mulling through his decreasing options, and poured the Jim Beam bourbon into the thick crystal glass before taking a lug, gratefully swallowing the burning liquid that eased down his throat. It gave him solace and, at the same time, courage. Courage for the decision he now knew he had to make.

CHAPTER 42

Frank sat still for a moment, letting it all sink in. He was half thinking of smoking a cigarette but quickly cast it out of his mind. He was proud of his whole month without having one.

"Is there anything you can tell us? It might not have seemed important at the time but could certainly help." Fowler said, studying Frank carefully. They sat in Detective Brown's office at the Royal Hong Kong police headquarters, where Frank had agreed to come back for questioning. He had been offered a deal by Brown which was; help with their investigation for which there would be no charges.

Frank had already covered everything he knew; his movements from Goa to Bangkok to Hong Kong. He told them who he had met from Richard Desmond to Theo Kampala and the Thai police chief—all of whom were now dead, except one, as far as he knew ... the man they called Mr Whiteman, who had seemed to be the brains behind the so-called drill. Whiteman was not one of the faces in the photographs strewn over the desk, most of which Frank had identified one by one. He leaned back slowly, feeling the fan cut through the air, chopping through its methodical rhythm.

Frank described Whiteman again, the silver-white hair, the aura of authority. "He said he worked for the Legislative Council of Hong Kong. The same crew Maria's Dad said he worked for."

Fowler exchanged a glance with Grant.

"You met Maria's father?" asked Fowler, cautiously.

"Yes, briefly. At her house, after the attacks," said Frank.

"You didn't mention that before," Grant frowned at him.

Frank shuffled in his chair with impatience. "I forgot. He gave me the passport contact; Li. Detective Brown, here, said Li was murdered."

"Will you excuse us for a moment?" said Fowler and the two men left the room, shutting the door behind them. Fowler shook his head and looked at the floor as Grant stared at him as though his world had just caved in around him.

"Are you thinking what I'm thinking, Ben?" Grant said quietly.

"What? That Cody is a Chinese plant?" Fowler couldn't bring himself to believe it. Cody had worked as an agent with the Hong Kong station for over ten years, his cover with the Legislative Council had been a perfect front. Now it seemed he had been using that position as a two-way channel with the Chinese.

"Yes, that he's the mole," Grant couldn't take his eyes off Fowler. Neither man wanted to believe it.

Frank sipped his black coffee from a paper cup and grimaced at the taste as he watched the two MI6 men outside behind the frosted glass. The pieces had all taken time to slot into place like a dovetailing line of parallel roads in his mind. There was something there, just out of grasp, its shape unclear as if a fog hung in front of him... Something Maria had said...

Detective Inspector Brown sat in the corner, where he had been observing the interview in a white shirt that stuck to his skin with the sleeves rolled up. He looked up at Frank, curiously, as if trying to read his thoughts.

The two intelligence officers re-entered the room and sat down in their seats, barely hiding their perplexed shock.

"Can I ask you a question?" Frank asked, glancing from Grant to Fowler. Fowler nodded.

"Does Peter Chapman – Maria's father – work for you, by any chance?" Again, the two men glanced at each other furtively.

"We can't answer that, I'm afraid. Confidential," answered Grant abruptly, focusing on a report in front of him.

"Because if he does," Frank leaned forward, "He's probably a good bet for being your mole."

Fowler stood up, banging his fist on the table. "How the hell do you know about a mole?" His voice was loud with barely restrained anger, but he was staring, wide-eyed, at the detective inspector. The Detective Inspector held out his hands in a defensive gesture. "What does it matter now? Are you going to find him or not?" he asked.

"The fact that we have a Chinese double agent in MI6 is a national security issue, Brown. And you tell a civvie?" He gestured towards Frank. "That was confidential information!" Fowler was yelling now, shaking with anger.

"This 'civvie' was framed by the Chinese, probably helped by your man!" Brown shouted, standing up as if to rise to the rage that seemed to be at boiling point in the room.

"That's enough!" barked Grant, who had been drumming his fingers on the desk throughout the confrontation. "We need to get over there."

"I'm coming with you," said Frank.

"No you're bloody not," retorted Fowler, who hadn't quite calmed down.

"He's with me and I'm going," said Brown, in a steady, low voice. Fowler shook his head in disbelief. "You're responsible for him, then. Grant, get some armed backup, in case."

CHAPTER 43

The blinds blocked out most of the light, shrouding a veil of darkness across the living room in which Peter Chapman sat in his favourite armchair. Hesitation and indecisiveness had clouded his mind in the previous few weeks. A suitcase, packed with his most treasured possessions, stood ready in the hallway, but he was unable to leave and wasn't even sure where he would go.

It had become obvious that his paymasters in Beijing had abandoned him to his fate and might even be considering killing him. That had closed off the option of defecting to the Chinese but, more importantly, there was Maria. The guilt of involving his beautiful daughter kneaded at his stomach like an untreated wound, growing more infected with every day that had passed since the attacks. He gulped another mouthful of Jim Beam and clunked the heavy crystal glass back on the side table.

A creak made him turn and his eyes blinked as if to reconfirm the sight of his daughter standing in the doorway.

"Dad?" her voice was quiet and uneven. He leapt up and went to her, his eyes welling with tears as he wrapped his arms around her. A huge wave of relief swept over him.

"Maria! Thank god you're alright. I thought I'd never see you again." She tried to speak, but a lump caught in her throat making her gulp. She looked up at him, her eyes filling with a wetness that dulled their usual emerald clarity. "Are you OK?"

Peter nodded and they moved into the room. He cleared a space on the sofa that was draped with clothes that he had previously been sifting through.

"I'm so sorry about everything. I need to tell you something," he said quietly. She perched gently on the leather sofa, looking around at the mess. It was a surprise to her as he always kept his house immaculate.

Peter sat next to her and breathed heavily as if preparing himself. "I did a terrible thing that you might not forgive me for. I wouldn't blame you. I'm not supposed to tell anyone, but I have been working for MI6 for over ten years." He paused, allowing Maria, who nodded grimly, to take it in before he hung his head and continued.

"Obviously there are serious consequences to me telling you this. But this is not the half of it. I've also been working for the Chinese MSS." Maria's eyes widened in surprise, her mouth remained closed.

"I was passing information to them regarding the 1997 takeover, as well as intelligence secrets. I had information on the recent attacks before they happened, no details though and I was not involved in the planning or anything like that. You have to believe me, Maria."

Maria squeezed her eyes shut as a tear ran slowly over her left cheek and then she got up suddenly and stood with her back to him.

"I had no way of stopping it or knowing the details of where it would take place. I did, however, pass the false information about the two lads," he paused, "Jimmy and your friend, Frank."

His daughter's face contorted with anguish, lower lip quivering uncontrollably. She gasped, suddenly desperate for air. "All those people...You knew?"

"I gave Beijing the information about Li Wu arranging a passport for Frank," Peter continued grimly as if his window of confession was about to close. "If it makes any difference, I had no idea they would track Frank down to your house. That mess with the killer. I would never have knowingly put you in danger, Maria. You have to believe that." He looked at her, pleadingly.

Maria looked up at the wall, tears streaming down her face, fixing her sight on an old colonial painting of Hong Kong harbour. She remembered it from when she was a little girl, like an old friend that anchored her to a happy childhood. Now it seemed to be cruelly taunting her as everything she thought she knew about her father was evaporating like some kind of mirage.

"So you met Frank at my house, gave him Li's information and then told the Chinese about Li. What did you think would happen then? You must have known they wanted to track Frank down and kill him?"

"I needed to give them something. They already knew that Frank had met you. There are always casualties in war," he said, as firmly as he could. "I didn't know everything that was going on, Maria, and I wanted to keep you out of it, to protect you!"

Maria snorted with derision as she paced up and down the room, shaking her head.

"Look, it's all been a shitty mess. I regret it all. You are the most important thing in my life. All I can do is apologise and ask that you forgive me, somehow," Peter said.

She looked at him through weeping eyes, shaking her head. "I don't know. I really don't know. I need time."

He looked at the floor. "Unfortunately that's something I don't have," he said quietly. A silence hung in the air, only the low background hum of the air conditioning filled the room.

"Do you remember when we were on the beach on a visit to Cornwall in England? You, me and your Mum... You were about five, I think. A boy was wandering around in the sand, crying his eyes out. He had completely lost his family and we looked after him for hours."

Maria stared at the blinds on the window, as if seeing the view of the city that lay behind them. She spoke quietly and smiled at the memory. "Yes, I do. I helped him build a huge sandcastle. You helped him calm down. You told him not to worry and that he'd see his mum again. You were always really caring like that," she said.

Peter breathed out heavily: "I'm still your father, Maria. Still your dad. The same man. Please don't remember me as anything else."

Maria glanced at the bottle of Jim Beam on the side table. "I think I need a drink. I'll get a glass."

"Maria," he looked across at her, the pain still very much apparent on his face. He held his hands out to her and she went to him. Peter Chapman held his daughter tightly for a moment and then looked into her eyes before nodding. "Go," he whispered, smiling faintly.

Maria stepped into the kitchen and opened the glass cabinet before grabbing a crystal whiskey glass. A distant thumping at the front door caused her to inhale quickly.

As Maria had left the room, Peter had walked to a mahogany wooden table in the corner and opened one of the drawers. Inside it was a Glock pistol that he had loaded before Maria had turned up, which he now picked it up in his sweaty hand. He knew that this was the only way. There was a high chance they would target Maria to get to him. If not, he would be hung out to dry in a long drawn out trial for treason, putting his family through hell.

He had shamed himself and nothing was going to change that. The banging at the front door seemed to focus him as if signalling that it was time.

The loud sound of the gunfire reverberated throughout the house, a shockwave that made Maria drop the glass, smashing it into hundreds of shards on the hard, marble tiled floor. A sickening horror careened through her body – as her legs automatically carried her back into the living room, glass cutting into the soles of her feet; pain she didn't feel or acknowledge – fear realised in the worst possible moment of her life as a daughter as she stared wide-eyed at the limp figure of her father, sprawled on the floor. Her mouth opened to scream without a sound as she scrambled onto her knees, pulling at his bloodstained shirt. Then an agonising wail shook at every wall in the house as if willing them to succumb to its force, closely followed by sudden loud crashes from the front door.

Benjamin Fowler inched into the room holding an automatic pistol, looking around as he took in the scene of agony, followed by Brown and Grant. Frank pushed past them and stood over Maria, who was desperately punching her father's chest.

"You don't get out of this that easy, you fucking bastard!"

Her whole body heaved with violent sobs as she shook her father by the shoulders as if willing him to wake up from a dream. His face was frozen by the impact of the bullet that had ripped through the back of his head. A splatter of brains, blood and sinew plastered the wall that had been behind him when he had taken his life a moment earlier.

"Jesus," Frank uttered and he leaned down to touch Maria's shoulder and comfort her. She ignored him and continued to clutch Peter's lifeless body.

Grant and Detective Inspector Brown were now in the room, looking down grimly at the tragedy that had just unfolded.

"Check out the rest of the house could you, Grant?" asked Fowler, quietly. His colleague nodded and disappeared out of the door. "Inspector Brown? Can you get your men to secure the perimeter, just as a precaution?"

Brown nodded and immediately turned to the sergeant who signalled his understanding and disappeared quickly from the room. Fowler circled round to get a better view of Peter's body and looked at Brown, sadly, as if to confirm that he was definitely dead.

CHAPTER 44

"Dean Whiteman was probably just an actor or a conman. Without a positive identification, it's hard to know, but we have the photo fit from your description on file, so you never know," Carl said.

Frank and Carl sat in the sunshine on the Victoria Embankment by the Thames, watching a large group of tourists clambering onto a ferry.

"I know you're close to Maria. She knew nothing about her father; the whole Hong Kong situation, and wasn't involved in any way."

Frank nodded. He had long stopped suspecting her of anything and now just felt incredible pain for her. He remembered Maria telling him that her dad had told her how much he loved her on the phone in Malaysia. He was probably saying goodbye, thinking he would never see her again.

"At least she got to see him," Frank said, continuing his own thoughts. "Before he topped himself, I mean." He sighed and shook his head. "What he was thinking, shooting himself like that?"

Carl patted Frank's shoulder sympathetically. "He was looking at a charge of treason. I guess he couldn't handle it. Perhaps, not mentally all there at the end."

Maria had said little since that horrendous incident a month previously. She'd given no hint on what her father had told her and Frank hadn't forced it, just repeating that he was there if she needed him.

"How is she?"

Frank shook his head again. "Not very well, I'm afraid. She needs time. She's with her mother in Amsterdam at the moment. She's mad at me, her Dad, she's…in a dark place. I'll go over there, soon. See if I can help. Got to do something."

Carl nodded and the two men stared out across the water, under a blue sky, as the tourist ferry passed them, slipping through the dark water.

"The part Peter Chapman played in this whole sorry affair will be kept under wraps by the Official Secrets Act, for now," said Carl as he stood up, clapping his gloved hands together.

"Come on, Frank. Let's walk along the river for a while."

PANDORA RED CHAPTER 1

March 1999. GCHQ Cheltenham, England.

Sarah Edwards glanced at the wall clock, noting it was 23:17 hours. Nearly time. The plan was to get started as the shifts changed to the night staff. During late shifts, the hexagon shaped green building, flanked by prison-like towers, had the feeling of a ship silently moving through the night. There was a faded sound, like a distant roar from outside the double glazed windows of her office, a downpour of rain Sarah could see coming down in sheets from an external building light.

The main GCHQ building was planted in the sprawl of the Oakley site in Cheltenham, England, where she had been an employee for 6 years. As Intelligence liaison officer, Sarah had access to top secret information that would never become public, even under the official secrets act. The glass walls of her office cast artificial light across the floor and she glanced outside into the main section area once again. A few people were still milling around, flickering screens showed worldwide operation updates, while the central heating hummed in the background. She moved her slight figure back into the large swivel chair and tapped once again on the screen, logging herself out of the main network. To access and copy the information meant using another terminal on the floor above.

Sarah cast her eyes around the office for the last time. The feeling weighed heavily that after tonight, she would possibly never see her family, her friends, or anyone she cared about again. She wouldn't be able to say goodbye either, that was the most painful part of it. For the last 3 months, she had churned the decision over and over in her mind and kept arriving at the same conclusion.

She put on her jacket, grabbed her bag, and slipped out across the thick carpet along the corridor, caged by metal and glass partitions that seemed to go on forever. Her feet quickly ascended the metal steps at the end, the echoes adding to her anxiety as she left G block and an entire lifetime behind her. No more after work drinks with the boys. No chinwags with her friend in the service, Janet Chambers. How surreal it would all soon seem.

She could only imagine the shock of her colleagues when the news spread about what she had done. They would understand, in time. Surely they would?

In a few years, this site would be empty of its machines, the people and the families in the housing complex would all be moved to the new GCHQ location at Benhall. The new 'doughnut' shaped complex would be state of the art at the cost of hundreds of millions and Sarah knew the security would be much tighter there, another reason to act now.

A quick flash of her identity card on the wall scanner and she was allowed through to the floor above. It would only be a matter of time before her access and subsequence actions were traced back to her but by then, all shit would have hit the fan and it wouldn't matter anymore.

Even now, it wasn't too late and she could still turn back. She could leave the building as normal and continue her life, keep her friends, and stay in touch with her family. She shook that idea out of her head quickly. This was no time for second thoughts or doubt. It seemed like a dream but she steeled herself and pressed on across the carpeted floor that hosted rows of cubicles, a haphazard mix of screens that flickered in the darkness as if watching her progress. The truth must be leaked, no matter what the consequences.

She stopped at a monitor, sat down, and quickly typed in her login and encrypted password to access the main system. There seemed to be a temporary freeze on the screen and Sarah frowned while she waited.

Access Denied flashed at her in large letters on the monitor.

She cursed under her breath. There was no logical reason she would be denied access at this level. Sarah retyped, her fingers stumbling across the keyboard, and she hit return to see the same 'Access Denied' once more.

Come on, Sarah, keep it together!

Slowly, she re-typed, voicing the letters and numbers in her head and breathed a sigh of relief as the familiar green coded access came up. She carefully plugged in the thumb drive that had been meticulously moulded to look like a keyless entry remote for a Honda Accord Acura TL, the exact same car she owned. It had been made through a contact that she had outside of the agency. Working with those outside the law had its benefits and discretion was essential.

She immediately hit the shortcut keys to launch the Shell access command line and typed in a sequence to bypass the computer's automatic security scan of her device.

Once again, she needed to fill in her login credentials to the remote server and then the black console screen filled with a fast moving list of file names as they copied from the 'Project Oculus' folder.

The same files that she had found and read with increasing alarm and exasperation over the previous months. She had not liked what she saw one bit.

"Good evening," the voice came from behind her, making her gasp out loud. Game over, before she had even started. The sounds of the footsteps grew nearer and she spun around, squinting at the night guard. He smiled at her, nodded, and walked on by. Sarah felt her heart pumping so loud, she was sure he could hear it. "Good evening," she replied.

Time slowed down, the file transfer was still reeling through its list and there was nothing Sarah could do to speed things up. There were a lot of files to copy.

She thought about her mother and father, seeing life drift by from their Brighton semi with a fine view of the sea and the pier. Had she really forsaken them? Would she really never see them again? Sarah refused to believe that. She would find a way.

She remembered first seeing the GCHQ advert in the newspaper. It was a test to find an apprentice and Sarah's mother had encouraged her to apply. Sarah had always been top of her classes, wiping the floor with everyone else and her future glittered like gold. But dark shadows loomed in the corners of her memory: the bullying. There were a few in her class who had targeted her. She could only guess it was because of her intelligence or maybe the social inadequacy.

The only thing she lived for was her studying, the knowledge that she so eagerly soaked up like a sponge and the books she buried herself in.

She passed the test, a puzzle to decode a series of seemingly random letters and then after a yearlong selection process, began her intelligence career, working in the foreign sources section and then later transferring to anti-terrorism monitoring.

It was at the 'firm' she met her first real friends. For the most part, anyway. There were a few comments from some of the male colleagues, but all in all, it was like a family. Besides, Sarah had always seen herself as a trailblazer, working hard to fight her way into a male-dominated environment.

A beep sounded and the copy was complete. She took the drive and slipped it inside her bag then typed in: *sfc /purgecache* in the command line to delete the cache and dump any record of her folder access before shutting down the workstation. She didn't want to leave unnecessary breadcrumb trails.

Sarah braced herself for getting out of the building. For obvious security reasons, no files of any kind were allowed to leave the walls of GCHQ. She knew the routine and just hoped she had thought of everything. There was a risk. There always was.

She moved quickly now, passing the endless monitors, workstations, and desks that seemed to blur past her. She rode the lift down to the ground floor, taking even, deep breaths to calm her nerves. The lift opened and she walked up to a set of double doors, passing her entry card over the scanner, which opened them with a gentle hiss.

Without hesitation, she stepped through and placed her leather handbag with the car key lob inside onto the x-ray scanner conveyor that was manned by Gilly, the elderly night security man. He smiled at Sarah and briefly glanced at the monitor that exposed the contents of her bag. It was a well-worn routine.

"It's a bit late for you, innit, love?" he asked in his thick welsh accent.

Sarah smiled weakly at him, the thumping in her chest once again seemingly growing louder with each beat as she brushed a strand of light brown hair behind her ear. "The devil's work is never done," she heard herself say. She stepped through the frame of a large metal detector, not unlike those in airports and held her breath as she did so, despite there being nothing incriminating on her person, the prospect of the alarm sounding haunted her. To her relief, no alarms were triggered and she stood at the end of the conveyor, waiting for her bag.

Gilly adjusted glasses on his wide face and scrutinised the monitor and shapes of items inside her bag; her purse, cosmetics, notepad, the Honda key-less entry remote...

He glanced at her for a moment, a hint of regret on his wrinkled face and sighed.

"I'm really sorry, luv, but I have to do a random check. You know how it goes."

Sarah stared at him for a second, half thinking he was joking and then realising he wasn't. She had only been subject to a couple of random checks in her whole time there and it had barely registered as a concern in her planning. Did he know something? It wasn't possible.

His face then turned to a grin, trying to make light of it. "It's your lucky night obviously."

Sarah then managed a smile in return but it was not good news. A random check meant a more thorough search and possibly a body check. The risk factor was rising.

"It's no problem. You've got a job to do," she said evenly.

The handbag came through and the guard began to take out the items one by one and place them on a table. Sarah fixed her eyes on the contents of her bag as he checked; looking inside the cosmetics pouch, flipping through the notepad at her meaningless scribbles. Most of the items had been placed in there for show; the plan always being to mix everything up in the bag. There were also random items such as food receipts or a tube of mints thrown in for good measure. She wondered if the cosmetics were overkill, especially as she barely ever wore much makeup.

His hands reached for the key lob and he picked it up, spinning it around in his fingers for a moment.

"Any weekend plans?" she asked, a forced cheery ring to her voice.

The guard turned and grinned again.

"At the allotment if it's not raining but we'll be lucky, won't we? It's bound to rain, innit?"

"Almost definitely," she said, clenching her fists inside her jacket pockets.

He sighed as if regretting something and began placing the items back in the bag and handed it to her.

"Have a lovely evening now," he said with finality. She took the bag and smiled in genuine relief. "You, too. Fingers crossed for the weather."

The rain-washed streets threw a cascade of reflections from the street lamps, the echo of Sarah's footfall bouncing off the walls of red-brick houses lining the complex where the GCHQ employees had built their lives. No one was out at that hour and a quietness hung in the air like a blanket.

No more friends.

She unlocked the front door to her cosy 2-bedroom semi where she had lived for almost 7 years.

No more family.

Grabbing the large holdall bag that waited in the hall, she then walked to her Honda Accord parked in the driveway and slung it into the boot. There was no point in going back to the house. Everything she could think of had been done, cleaned down, or shredded. Anything she had not wanted them to find had been taken to the landfill, 5 miles away. Her entire life was now in one bag.

The car weaved its way past the red brick houses and grey block buildings, away from the complex and toward Cheltenham train station.

Frank was running across the underground concourse, weaving over the charred bodies, victims of some kind of fire. Their dark shapes seemed to melt into the polished marble floor and the inky black liquid congealed around his feet, making it more and more difficult to run. His pursuer's heavy breathing was close behind, yet he dared not look.

The lift service hatch was just ahead, yellow and black stripes beckoning – his escape route clearly marked. And now, worse still, the arms of the dead, constrained by the dark liquid, seemed to move and reach for him, their bony blackened hands gripping at his legs and feet. Frank's heart pumped hard in his chest and it was difficult to breathe as if air was been sucked right out of his lungs.

To his horror, the service door began to slowly close with an eerie scraping sound, like the echo of train tracks in a distant tunnel.

Five feet away.

He had to get there. Kicking away the clinging hands, Frank accidentally stood on a body, the sickening crunch of brittle bones sounded underfoot but he ignored it, striving on through the sticky residue.

Four feet away.

The doors ground closer together like a slowly snapping jaw. With a leap, Frank threw himself forward with all his energy, hands clambering to hold them open so he could lever his body forward. Somehow, he found strength again and hauled himself forward over the slippery floor and into the lift. As the doors closed behind him, he caught a glimpse of the bodies of the dead crawling after him and that of his pursuer, who had now become one of them, burnt black and red, the skin falling away from his flesh. Staring right at him through sunken sockets was the unmistakeable bloodied face of Chiu Wah, the assassin he had thrown out of a train eight years earlier.

The sheets, soaked from sweat, were wrapped tightly around him as Frank fought to free himself, breathing hard and disorientated. He knocked the side table, pushing a glass of water to the floor, which cracked and rolled, soaking the carpet and his unread books.

"Jesus," he muttered, untangling himself. The bed looked like he had been wrestling with an army of demons. Pillows were strewn over the floor, the sheet lay twisted across the mattress. He rubbed his eyes and slowed his breathing, relieved that the nightmare was over. Every now and then, it would re-appear and he wondered why. It had been so long since Hong Kong and there had been many other demons to fight afterwards.

Frank switched on the radio and padded his naked frame over to the en-suite bathroom before turning on the shower, hesitating at the door until the water had a chance to heat up.

After a quick blast and scrub, he dried himself, checked his unshaven face and dark hair in the mirror, and threw on a T-shirt and jeans. He headed down the hallway to the kitchen and opened the fridge, glancing into the bare interior. Had Maria asked him to get the shopping in? She had been talking to him when he was half asleep that morning, which was always a bad idea. Where was she anyway? Then he remembered that she had taken the boys to see a friend and then get shopping.

A dull pain throbbed in the back of his skull but he still didn't hesitate to grab the last can of beer.

It had been a difficult reunion after Hong Kong and the horrific suicide of her father. They had been sitting in a café on Amsterdam's Raadhuisstraat two months after her father's funeral, watching the rain hammer the streets and trams trundle by the window. Maria had avoided his eyes as he uttered sympathetic words and he knew they weren't getting through. They had something, hadn't they? They'd been together under the threat of death and helped each other through those terrifying weeks that neither would easily forget.

Then it had happened. The gunshot in the living room. The sight of her dad lying on the Chinese rug, the blood and brain tissue marking it like a chaotic map.

"You blame me, don't you?" he had said. "If I had never come into your life, maybe it wouldn't have turned out like that. Is that what you think?" She shook her head, brushed a hand through her curly blonde hair, but said nothing and continued to stare at the rain, or was it his reflection in the window? He couldn't be sure.

"Of course I don't blame you, Frank. I just don't know where I am right now. I'm all lost," she said without looking at him, her green eyes seemed duller than he remembered. He tried to take her hand but she moved it too soon and they sat in silence for a while as the coffee machine growled out another customer's Americano.

He gave her his new contact card, carefully placing it on the table. When she didn't acknowledge it, he stood up, scraping the chair on the stone floor.

"Just call when you're ready," he said quietly as he followed her gaze out into the rain. "If you need to," he added.

It was too soon for her to pick up any thread they'd had in Asia. That much was obvious. She needed more time but he feared losing her. The chance of never seeing her bright green eyes and freckled face again cast a shadow over his thoughts.

Frank left the café, running for the tram in the hacking downpour, convinced he would never see her again. He certainly didn't envisage that Maria would contact him only a week later with the news that would change his life forever. The news that she was pregnant.

Adventure. Breaking up the boredom. The fact that he was certain the relationship with Maria was over. There were many reasons Frank agreed to join Carl at MI6 after he had returned from Asia.

The dark truth was he had also experienced a real adrenaline buzz throwing the Chinese assassin from that train in Thailand. And with his death, knowing the killer would never try to kill him or Maria again, just put the icing on the cake. He got the job done. Dead was dead. There was no coming back from death. Except in your dreams. Frank smiled at the irony.

Death. Once you let it pervade your life, it took a hold, became 'normal', a way of dealing with things. Something changed in Frank after that killing. He had become a different beast and knew it. A beast capable of darker acts. Kill or be killed.

No more office job B.S. No more being the hamster in a wheel, a wage slave just existing to work. No, he was going to grab this and run with it. Run bloody fast.

Adventure, excitement, travel. That was what had driven him before. Now? Now he had responsibilities. He needed to build a safety net. A home.

Frank nursed his beer in the stark living room and flicked to the news where footage of Riot police and demonstrators clashed in Seattle. He watched impassively as police charged the line, petrol bombs stinging the air as batons pounded heads and limbs before the newsreader moved the story quickly on, his mind still wandering.

Maria did love him now, he knew that more than words could ever describe. When she said she was pregnant, everything had changed. Then Joe had come along, and now they had Zak as well. As the news continued, Frank wondered what kind of world he had brought his children into.

Pandora Red by Jay Tinsiano. (Frank Bowen #2)
ISBN: 978-1-9997232-3-1

Frank Bowen's mission is to find a GCHQ whistleblower but in doing so unwittingly risks everything, including his own family's safety.

As part of a covert team, assigned to dangerous missions, Bowen believes he knows what he's up against until a team of Russian mercenaries are thrown into the mix, leaving everyone and everything hanging in the balance.

It's a race against the clock to save all that he holds dear and uncover the dark truths behind his mission.

White Horse by Jay Tinsiano and Jay Newton. (Dark Paradigm #1)
ISBN: 978-1-9997232-1-7

Half a world away in Spain and running from his past, a Los Angeles gangster unwittingly takes a train that's headed straight into a terrorist attack. He survives only to face an even deadlier threat.

On that same train: a virologist with clues to a deadly epidemic. Did his secrets die with him in the strike?

Raging in the aftermath, a foul-tempered police chief with a daughter caught in the attack thirsts for revenge. But against whom?

An orphan child without a name disappears down a dark, illegal CIA mind-control programme. Now trained in the ways of death, he prepares to do his master's twisted bidding.

From its first pages, the relentless techno-thriller White

Horse drops you with a thunderclap in the middle of these colliding worlds. This tale of global conspiracy that threatens humanity itself will keep you guessing whether anyone can survive.

For more information on the full catalogue visit: **www.jaytinsiano.com**

NEWSLETTER

To join the VIP Jay Tinsiano reading group head to:
www.jaytinsiano.com/newsletter

- Free Books and stories
- Previews and Sneak Peeks
- Exclusive material

ABOUT THE AUTHOR

Jay Tinsiano is a keen traveller and has recently based himself in the Dominican Republic, Colombia and Europe while writing his latest books.

Jay is also an avid reader and writer of fiction, specifically crime, sci-fi and thrillers and interweaves his experiences into his fiction writing.

If you enjoyed reading False Flag please do consider leaving a review on the platform you purchased it. Not only do reviews help and support Jay write more books they are also essential for acceptance to book promotion programmes that help him find new readers.

Thanks again,